THE COMPLETE EXPLOITS OF

THE NOTORIOUS SEA FOX

THE COMPLETE EXPLOITS

OF THE NOTORIOUS

SEA FOX

JAMES K. WATERMAN

INTRODUCTION BY

JAMES REASONER

ALTUS PRESS • 2022

TABLE OF CONTENTS

INTRODUCTION

BY JAMES REASONER

I'VE ALWAYS taken a fairly simple approach to reading pulp stories: I try to put myself in the same mindset as the stories' original audience, as if I'd had a dime burning a hole in my pocket and just picked up the latest issue of *Western Story* or *Dime Detective* or *Argosy*, so I could settle down in my favorite reading chair and enjoy an exciting yarn.

Of course, we can do that only to a certain extent. We can't just put aside completely our own experiences and beliefs. We're not living in the 1920s, '30s, or '40s. But I think it's worthwhile to keep in mind that the pulp stories we love were written in a time when many things were totally different than they are today, and expecting them to read as if they were written now is a mistake.

That attitude is why we can read a story like Jack Williamson's "Born of the Sun," originally published in the March 1934 issue of *Astounding Stories*, and enjoy it despite the rather far-fetched scientific ideas it contains. (And the central one is a doozy, so if you haven't read the story, I won't spoil it for you!) We can't expect today's level of scientific accuracy from stories written eighty or ninety years ago.

Likewise, we can read an issue of *Private Detective* and enjoy a story where a beautiful dame ankles into the private eye's office and interrupts his drinking to dump a load of trouble in his lap. Or an issue of *Star Western* where the lead novel features a stalwart cowboy hero saving the ranch from rustlers and winning the love of the rancher's beautiful daughter. Have we seen that stuff before? Sure, we have. Enough times that some might call them clichés. But they weren't clichés in 1938, at least not to the extent they are now, and reminding myself of that and putting myself in the place of the readers who bought those issues at the newsstands helps increase my enjoyment of reading them now.

Sometimes taking that attitude is difficult. Some pulp reprints carry a disclaimer on the copyright page. Something like "These pulp stories were written in a different era and contain attitudes, language, and cultural depictions which may cause offense today." This is just a reminder not to judge the stories too harshly, or to apply our modern standards to them too stringently, because it's unrealistic to expect fiction written so long ago to live up to such standards. An acceptance and understanding of that concept makes it possible for us to read and enjoy stories shaped by points of view in which most people no longer believe.

And then… along comes something like the Sea Fox series by James K. Waterman.

JAMES K. WATERMAN was an American author, born in Boston, with a background as a sailor on whaling ships and in the merchant marine, as well as working as a journalist, before turning to fiction. Between 1922 and 1929, he wrote approximately two dozen stories of nautical adventure for the pulps, his output split between *The Frontier, Adventure,* and *Sea Stories.* He doesn't appear to have written any novels, and he disappears from the pulps after 1929. An obscure author, to be sure, but while he was writing, he turned out a series unlike anything else I've ever encountered.

Simply put, the hero of the Sea Fox stories is a slave trader.

Cap'n Barnabas N. Pepper is the master of the brigantine *Wild Pigeon,* which plies the waters of the Atlantic between the west coast of Africa and the east coast of the United States, in the years before the American Civil War. Pepper is one of the most successful slave ship captains, which means the American and British navies devote considerable effort toward catching him. He's assisted by his first mate, Tom Dollar, and a giant black bosun known as Robin Hood.

The idea that a slave trader could be the hero of a pulp series is more than a little off-putting, even for the 1920s. Waterman seems to be aware of this and tries to mitigate it by stating plainly that Cap'n Pepper is widely regarded as the most humane of the slave ship captains. Indeed, Pepper risks his own life to save several hundred slaves from being blown up when they're imprisoned in a ship rigged with a bomb to explode. He's smart, loyal to his friends and allies, and operates on a strict code of honor. Indeed, if he were smuggling anything other than human beings, chances are the readers would regard him as a lovable rogue and have no trouble rooting for him. This seems to be exactly the sort of character Waterman was trying to create.

So, in reading these stories, the question becomes whether the reader can put aside the part of Pepper's personality that makes him engage in this activity and concentrate on his more admirable qualities.

I've been reading a great deal of war fiction lately, and one subgenre that's proven popular over the years is that of "the good German." These are stories and novels written from the point of view of German soldiers, usually enlisted men or non-coms, but sometimes officers. One of the earliest examples is Erich Maria Remarque's novel *All Quiet on the Western Front*, and the trope shows up again in novel series by Sven Hassel, Leo Kessler (Charles Whiting), and Bruno Krauss (Kenneth Bulmer), among others. Even though the central characters in these stories are fighting on what we now consider the wrong side, we're able to accept them as protagonists because of the admirable personal qualities they bring to the table. They may possess a fatal flaw, but that doesn't damn them entirely in our eyes.

I think it's possible to approach the Sea Fox stories in the same way. The slave trade existed; that's historical fact. I can accept it as such and read these stories as well-written, exciting nautical adventure yarns. Over the course of seven stories, Cap'n Pepper battles rival slavers who are worse than he is, dodges efforts by the American, British, and French to capture him, rescues a kidnapped girl, befriends an American commodore and saves his life, and even assumes temporary command of an American naval vessel. Waterman's background as a sailor gives these stories an undeniable air of authenticity, and the plot twists he brings to them are clever and unexpected. It's easy to imagine that readers of the 1920s (some of whom probably remembered the Civil War) would accept and enjoy them.

The readers of a hundred years later will have to decide that for themselves. The Sea Fox series provides a vivid window into a long-gone era and does so by presenting stirring tales of courage and action, and as a series unlike anything else in the pulps, I believe they're worth reading.

THE SEA FOX

Many a British and American naval officer ranged the West African coast in vain trying to trap the wily Sea Fox. Then Commander Gregory took a hand in the game—and so did the Portuguese slaver, Taveira

"**N**OW WHAT in Tophet d'yer suppose that shiver-the-mizzen-lookin' cuss is a-doin' up in that tree this early in the mornin'?" the captain asked himself, fingering his scraggly sun-bleached mustache and goatee thoughtfully. "Looks mighty suspicious to me, somehow."

Cap'n Barnabas N. Pepper, better known as "The Sea Fox" along that 1,500 mile stretch of humid, miasmatic, West African coast between Rio Pongo and Old Calabar, was returning to his ship this Fourth of July morning, after attending an all-night native revel as a guest of the King of Bonny. Suddenly, dazzling, intermittent flashes of light emanating from a lone cotton-tree arrested his attention. This towering tree stood about fifty yards distant from the west bank of the sluggish Bonny River. In the top branches, seventy-five feet from the ground, was a stout platform provided with a seat and thatched with palm-leaves as a protection from sun and rain. This was the slavers' lookout station. Before proceeding down the river the Captain of a slaver invariably sent a man up there to see if any cruisers were hovering outside the bar at the mouth of the river.

What had elicited the startled observation from the captain was the startling discovery that the platform was now occupied by an entirely different type of person from that for which it had been erected. Instead of the eagle-eyed, weatherbeaten slaver carelessly dressed in dungaree trousers and hickory shirt, a trim figure of a man garbed in the neat duck uniform of an American

1

navy sailor now occupied the lookout. Moreover, this interloper, unaware of the captain's presence, was calmly heliographing, by means of a small pocket-mirror, to some party or parties outside of Cap'n Pepper's field of observation. Needless to say, the Sea Fox was not a little disturbed at these furtive tactics which one of his natural enemies was carrying on under, or rather over, his very nose.

Accordingly Cap'n Pepper planted his short, square figure firmly, elevated his stubby, freckled nose high in the air and, jerking out a pocket pistol, drew a bead on the signaler.

"Come down outa that, you!" he bellowed. "Come down quick before ye come down head first!"

The man-of-war's man looked down, grinned, and, pocketing the mirror, swung onto the Jacob's-ladder, his tall, well-knit form swaying from side to side as he descended with an ease betokening long familiarity with ladders of that pattern slung over a ship's side. He landed lightly on the ground before the captain, the arched nostrils of his large aquiline nose lifting slightly in a smile; his cool, gray eyes regarding the other's snapping black ones unperturbedly.

"Captain Pepper, I presume," he remarked blithely. "I must say you're an early riser, sir, especially on a holiday. This is the glorious Fourth, you know."

The Sea Fox glowered, taking in at a glance the stranger's demeanor, unmistakably that of an officer and a gentleman.

" 'Bout thirty years old, I'd say, an' nothin' less than a leftenant I'll bet my hat," was the captain's mental appraisment. Aloud he barked: "T'hell with that palaver. What ye doin' up there with that lookin'-glass is what I wanta know." He menaced with the pistol.

"Why, I don't mind telling you, Captain," returned the other sweetly. "I was communicating with the United States Brig-of-war *Porpoise*. She's hove-to outside the bar."

"The *Porpoise!*" repeated Cap'n Pepper with a grimace of dismay. "Confound that Commodore Gregory to hell. As soon's

I arrived on the coast this voyage I was warned to keep a weather eye liftin' for him. Can't be possible he's here this quick. I heard only yesterday that he was a hundred an' eighty miles to the nor'west of here; off Benin or nigh to it."

"Your scouts evidently aren't as reliable as ours, Captain. The *Porpoise* is here and two more of Commodore Gregory's squadron, the *Bainbridge* and the *Perry,* are cruising close at hand in the Bight of Biafra."

The manner in which the navy man imparted this information showed that he was not at all displeased that they had finally cornered the Sea Fox, whose strategic artifices, combined with the swift-sailing qualities of his brigantine, the *Wild Pigeon,* had long been the despair of the American and English cruisers.

"Close at hand, eh? Well, be damned to 'em. It's the *Porpoise* I'm considerin' now. What was you a-tellin' 'em with that glass, I'd like to know?"

"I was telling them that there was a mighty fine slaving brigantine lying concealed in that thick grove of mangroves and kanana trees, by the river bank there. I had some difficulty in making her out, too. She was so cleverly disguised with those branches of trees lashed to her trucks and upper spars."

"And you never would have detected her either," declared Cap'n Pepper with a flash of pride at his handiwork, "if some of them sore-head Fantees hadn't told ye where to look." He paused and deftly patted the other's clothing in a search for weapons.

"I had a pistol," the navy man stated, "but I lost it somehow coming through the brush before daylight this morning."

"You did, eh," grunted the captain. "Well, you can see plain enough I ain't lost mine an' the *Porpoise* is a-goin' to be an officer short if you don't skip aloft there right now an' signal your ship that you mistook some of them trees for the masts of my vessel. Them seaman's togs you're wearin' don't fool a bit. Up ye go!"

The navy man shook his head.

"It's positively no use for me to do that, Captain," he stated calmly, "because the commodore knows beyond the question of a doubt that the *Wild Pigeon* is lying here with two hundred and five slaves aboard. I was merely detailed to signal the course for our boats to take. There are three boats now just behind that curve in the river. They carry forty-five men and each boat mounts a four-pound swivel. You can see they got you this time, Captain. You—"

The Sea Fox waited to hear no more. He wheeled and was off on the run for his ship, with the navy man close at his heels. "It's no use, Captain. Be sensible. Game's up," the latter panted.

Cap'n Pepper's feet chugged along the sedgy shore of the river until he came to the bamboo landing to which his beautiful craft was made fast. He was bounding along this landing when his straining eyes caught sight of the three boats, crammed with man-of-war's men, pulling around a turn in the bank and within easy hailing distance of his ship. He cursed between his teeth as he thought of losing the two hundred and five slaves now below her deck. They were the pick of the Aro nation, the finest specimens of black humanity he had ever seen in his twenty years of slaving. Among them were fifty-three fine, strapping girls, anywhere from seventeen to twenty years old, that he had procured after much hazardous labor from the priest of the "Long Juju" (sacred grove) at Aro-Chuku. These comely girls would fetch from five to eight hundred dollars a piece as maids for some of the stately mansions of Virginia.

What counted even more with the Sea Fox, as with every

true sailor, was the idea of losing his splendid brigantine. Hers was the swiftest keel that ever parted the waters of the Gulf of Guinea, as many a wrathful man-of-war officer to whom she had flaunted a saucy stern, flying westward, could testify. Never, the captain felt, would he be able to get her like again.

The *Porpoise's* boats would have reached the *Wild Pigeon* at about the same time as her captain but for a startling and totally unexpected interruption. Suddenly a wild-eyed, red-shirted son of the State of Delaware boiled up through the after companion-scuttle, a lighted match flaring like a torch in his hand. This effervescent mariner was the chief officer, Mr. Tom Dollar and, being nearly as blind as an owl with drink, he saw nothing of the approaching boats.

Bounding to the long twelve-pounder at the stern, he slapped the match to the touch-hole. Followed a roar that rent the quiet air and set the monkeys to jabbering for miles along the river banks; a double-headed shot raked the bank of port oar-blades of the head boat, cutting them as cleanly as a knife and upsetting some of the oarsmen.

"Hoo-roo—hoo-roo fur the Fourth o' July!" screeched Tom Dollar.

With a neighing laugh, he spun half-way round and collapsed at the breech of the gun, where he immediately began snoring raucously.

CAP'N PEPPER ripped out an oath of vexation.

"Ain't that just plumb hell!" he growled to the navy man. "If that crazy Tom Dollar has killed any of your party it means a Federal prison for life, that is if we ain't hanged. What's your name, mister?"

"Candage," answered the other. "Luke Candage."

"Well, Mr. Candage, I may want ye for a witness one of these days. You must have seen that my mate was drunk an' didn't know what he was doin'. I'll see there's no more o' that business goin' on."

He rushed up the gangway and down into the cabin, expecting to find a hilarious drinking party there. Much to his surprise the cabin was deserted. His roving eyes finally lighted on a white sheet of paper scrawled over with writing and pinned to the table with the thin-bladed knife he used to cut up tobacco. It was written in Spanish, a language the captain could read and write fluently, but he had no time to read it now; the tramp of feet sounded on the companion-way and he had barely shoved the note into his pocket when Mr. Candage came in with the officer in charge of the boarding party.

"Good morning, Captain," greeted the officer, who wore the epaulets of a lieutenant. "Mr. Candage here has explained that your twelve-pounder was fired just now merely to commemorate the Fourth and not with any designs against us. Your mate was a little reckless but as there's nobody hurt we'll say no more about it. I want to take a look around your vessel, Captain, just to satisfy myself as to her real character."

Cap'n Pepper, knowing the futility of protesting against this search of his vessel, smiled and handed over his keys.

"Go as far as you like, gentlemen," he told them and, picking his pipe from the table, filled and lighted it unconcernedly.

From his coolness one would never suspect that the fifty-three girls were quartered in the long rooms on each side of the cabin.

In the next five minutes the lieutenant discovered, much to his astonishment and, needless to say, Cap'n Pepper's, that these rooms were now destitute of anything in the shape of a human being. The girls had vanished.

A search of the hold, clean, roomy, well-lighted by glass cones set into the deck and ventilated by wind-sails in the hatches, also proved fruitless. The one hundred and fifty-two male slaves quartered there were now missing, as if they had dissolved in thin air.

The *Wild Pigeon* was a slaver *de luxe*. She laid no slave-decks, nor did she carry leg-irons, "middle-chains," or any other device for manacling slaves.

After an examination of the ship's papers, which were strictly in form, the lieutenant knew that he had no grounds for holding the vessel. He had had his trouble for nothing.

"Well, I am astonished, most damnably astonished," he declared with a look of mingled chagrin and admiration at Cap'n Pepper. "We know positively that you had over two hundred slaves aboard here at six o'clock last night and we would have been here long before this if the bar hadn't been so rough before the tide turned. What you've done with the slaves I don't know, but I can see that your nickname is most appropriate. You have all the attributes of old Reynard, but don't forget, Captain, we'll be waiting off the bar for you to come out. We haven't given up hope of getting you by any means. Good day."

He went over the rail, leaving Cap'n Pepper standing there fingering his goatee in a bewildered manner. In all truth, he was as much at a loss as the lieutenant to account for the disappearance of his slaves, but he had a feeling that the note which all along had been burning a hole in his pocket, so to speak, would shed some light on the mystery. As soon as the naval contingent was well on its way down the river he drew back under the awning and in a twinkling his eyes were flaming over the written sheet. It ran:

To the Sea Fox:
    I have had much trouble in filling up my ship with a slave-cargo and so, finding a goodly number aboard of your vessel, I took great pleasure in helping myself to them. How I did it is for you to find out. But by the time you get clear of the Porpoise *I shall have completed loading at Forcados River and be bound home.*
                           Captain Rosenda Taveira,
                                Schooner Toreador.
P.S. My knife is stuck in your mainmast. R. T.

THE SEA FOX, his heavy jaw protruding, each stubbly hair of his mustache and goatee bristling with rage, leaped to the mainmast and jerked out the leather-hafted, narrow-bladed knife sticking there. According to slaving custom a knife planted in the mainmast of a rival conveyed an unmentionable insult, an insult which it was understood must be wiped out in no other way than by sheathing the blade in the owner's heart. Cap'n Pepper looked at the knife a long moment and then threw it into the river. He rarely worked along established lines. He would have revenge on Taveira in his own way; and he knew he was going to have his work cut out for him before he squared accounts with this scourge of the slave coast.

"Panyerer" (Kidnapper) Taveira feared neither God, man, nor the devil. He snapped his fingers at the cruisers and, in the slavers' resorts along the Mole in Havana, boasted with great gusto of how, when once he was pursued by a man-of-war and capture seemed imminent he had shackled the sixty slaves he had aboard at the time to heavy chains and grouped them on the weather side of the after-house. Then suddenly jibing his mainsail, the heavy boom had knocked them kicking into the sea, thus removing all evidence from the eyes of the baffled searching party that had boarded him an hour later.

This hunch-backed, horse-faced, one-eyed Portuguese monster swore that he would never be taken alive. At all times there was a fuse leading from a drawer in the desk at the head of his berth down to the powder-magazine of his schooner.

"Me, my niggers, and those navy dogs will all go to hell at the same time the moment I see a boarding-party routing my crew," he bragged in his drinking bouts, his black, bushy brows lifting in a ferocious leer.

Cap'n Pepper fetched a deep sigh at the thought of all his splendid black people now crammed, with not so much room as a man in his coffin, between the sweltering, loathsome decks of the *Toreador*, entirely at the mercy of this inhuman captain.

True, Taveira, by stealing his slaves, had saved the Sea Fox from having his vessel and cargo confiscated and relieved him of the necessity of forfeiting three thousand dollars bail, the customary amount fixed by the United States Judge in such cases. But rather a hundred times would he have undergone that ordeal than to have had that diabolical Taveira take the wind out of his sails in such a manner. This feeling was not diminished when presently the captain discovered that Taveira had not only taken his slaves but had also carried off his bosun, Robin Hood, a freeborn Negro from Massachusetts and without his equal as a seaman.

"Come, get into gear here!" growled Cap'n Pepper, a few minutes later, shaking Tom Dollar by the collar. "Every man-jack forrad is stretched out like a dead herrin'. Just a-reekin' of rum an' laudanum they be, an' it looks like ye got plenty of the same dose. Wake up an' tell me what that cussed Portygee done to ye all."

The mate partly opened one eye.

"Hoo-roo—for Fourth—J'ly!" he muttered feebly, and, slowly closing the eye, began snoring again.

"Well, the Fourth prompted ye to do one good trick anyway," grumbled the captain, surveying the disheveled figure of his mate disgustedly. "By firing that gun ye stopped the lieutenant long enough for me to get Taveira's note outa the way before he clapped eyes on it. 'Twould interfere with my plans if the *Porpoise* knew where my slaves had gone to."

Going to the galley, the captain built a fire and made a large kettle of strong black coffee. Then he dumped a can of mustard into a two-quart pitcher of warm water and was stirring it with an iron spoon when four of the crew who had spent the night ashore somewhere, came over the rail.

These men Cap'n Pepper at once converted into nurses. With loud guffaws they began dosing their shipmates with the stinging emetic. The mustard and coffee worked wonders and in the course of an hour the mate and crew had come to life and were wabbling about the decks.

Their rather incoherent version of the affair finally simmered down to the fact that the Mandingo cook, whom the captain had shipped that week before in Old Calabar, was merely a tool of Taveira's. It was the cook who had brought four bottles of rum to the foremost hands to celebrate the night before the Fourth. The patriotic Tom Dollar had fallen for the same bait.

A search of the cook's bunk showed that he had gone with his master and taken all his belongings.

Cap'n Pepper could visualize quite easily just how Taveira had pulled the trick. The cook must have sent word to the Portuguese that Cap'n Pepper would be absent from his vessel that night; he himself had told the cook that he was going to the king's Chop-day celebration. The fact that there was a United States cruiser off the mouth of the river had proved no deterrent to the piratical slaver.

Seven miles up the Bonny River was a creek eight miles long which emptied into the Andoni River. The mouths of the rivers were fourteen miles apart and, if the existence of the creek was known to the *Porpoise,* which was doubtful, it was not considered navigable for any slave craft.

All had been plain sailing for Taveira. He had simply anchored his light-draft schooner at the Andoni end of the creek and removed the *Wild Pigeon's* slaves with his boats.

THERE AIN'T no two ways 'bout it, Cap'n. That yallerbelly has hooked us sunthin' scand'lous," observed Tom Dollar, rubbing his aching head dejectedly. "One thing is certain: he ain't going to no Forcados River like he says in the note. He's just settin' ye a false course case ye go to follerin' him. He'll likely go the other way; p'raps as far south as Ambriz an' finish loadin'. What ye goin' to do now, Cap'n?"

"Do? Why I'm a-goin' to get my niggers back if I have to follow the *Toreador* clear to Cuby. I'd be the laffin' stock of the coast if Taveira gets away with 'em. It's my opinion that he's got his load and is off on the 'Middle Passage' right now. If he was intendin' to remain longer on the coast it ain't likely he'd a-bothered us. Well, we'll go after him. We got to get busy. My doctor book says in a case o' laudanum pizenin' to give 'em emetics an' strong coffee an' forced, prolonged, an' active exercise. I've given ye the first two an' now we'll have the rest. This ship has got to be ready for haulin' through the creek by nightfall. So turn all hands to an' get everythin' shipshape an' Bristol fashion."

A little after dark the tired, sweaty crew, by means of running-lines made fast to trees along the banks, began warping their ship through the creek connecting the two rivers. It was man-killing labor, for part of the way they literally had to force her sharp keel through the slimy mud of the creek bottom. The air in that black, narrow ribbon of water, between dense growth of mangroves and tropical plants of immense size, was as dead and nearly as hot as the inside of a furnace.

The monkeys scolded and the jump-fish croaked at this unusual disturbance of their habitat. Now and then the long yardarms of the vessel would rip through some rank foliage and scatter leaves on the deck, many of them quite large enough to have made an overcoat. There was no moon, but the great stars blazed out like electric lights set in a vast velvet canopy, giving light enough for sailors to work.

By 4:30 in the morning they were through the creek. After all hands had "spliced the main brace" with a double portion of grog, sail was made and, with a heavy squall commingled with rain and lightning sweeping over her stern, the *Wild Pigeon* darted down the Andoni River nearly as fast as the beautiful bird whose name she bore.

At dawn they crossed the bar and stood out into the Bight, steering a southerly course to get well clear of the land and to avoid the *Porpoise,* which at that moment was lying off the Bonny River, well within the hundred-fathom curve her officers congratulating themselves on having the wary Sea Fox tightly bottled up.

"By crickety! This is one time we've wiped Commodore Gregory's eye," chuckled Cap'n Pepper to his mate as they stood watching the sun shoot above the inshore mist. "We've fooled him completely."

"I believe you have. I'm quite sure the commodore never anticipated this," interrupted a laughing voice.

Wheeling, the slavers beheld, in the companion-scuttle, the smiling face of Mr. Candage.

"Where the hell did ye come from?" the Sea Fox blurted out, striding toward him with mouth agape.

Mr. Candage emerged from the companion and seated himself coolly on the edge of the skylight as if his being there was the most natural thing in the world, his smile deepening as if well pleased with himself and all around him. This smile was so irresistibly contagious that Cap'n Pepper's stern features relaxed visibly, while Tom Dollar showed his tobacco-stained teeth in a wide grin.

"It's rather cramped quarters down in your storeroom," observed the newcomer, "so I came on deck to stretch my legs a bit."

Briefly he told them that he had been detailed to keep an eye on the *Wild Pigeon* as it was suspected that her slaves had merely been removed temporarily to one of the barracoons near Bonny. When he had seen the slaver about to haul through the creek he had slipped alongside in a canoe and, under cover of darkness, had gained the storeroom without being observed.

"Looks as though my zeal has made me overshoot the mark," he laughed. "I can assure you, Captain, that I had no intention of going to sea with you."

"Yes, seems like ye got yourself in quite a mess, Mr. Candage," replied the Sea Fox. "The simplest way for us to get ye outa it would be to knock ye on the head right now an' throw ye over the side. D'yer know that?"

"Perfectly well, Captain. But I also know you'd never do it. You're not that kind. You don't kill in cold blood. You have the reputation among us navy men of being the most humane slaver in these seas."

"That might all be," returned the Sea Fox. "Them guns we carry ain't for fightin' you folks"—he smiled grimly—"but to protect us from our own kind. There may be some sorta honor among thieves, but there ain't none with slavers—the Portygee kind anyway. Now tell me, Mr. Candage, what was ye aboard the *Porpoise?*"

"I—I held the rank of lieutenant, Captain."

"H-m, I thought so. Well, I don't want to be too strict with ye, an' I'll put you on parole if you'll give me your word that ye won't do nothin' to the detriment of my ship or crew while you're aboard here. You can see 'twould be mighty inconvenient for us if ye should start cuttin' the braces or halliards when some of your cruisers was a-chasin' us."

"Very well," Mr. Candage decided, after a moment's thought. "I give you my word that I'll do nothing to endanger your ship or crew while I'm aboard here. And I also promise that when you're my prisoner I'll extend to you a similar courtesy."

"I b'lieve you. But I ain't anxious to test your hospital'ty just now, Leftenant," chuckled Cap'n Pepper, pleased to find the navy man such a likeable chap. "Now just make yourself at home. If I ain't forgot my hull bag o' tricks I reckon before long you'll see more real, hell-for-leather excitement with this here craft in one hour than ye would on the *Porpoise* in a month o' Sundays."

THE *WILD PIGEON* was steering the course of a slaver bound to Cuba, and thirty-six hours from the time she crossed the bar she sighted on the horizon, square in the middle of the setting sun, the tops'ls of a schooner.

"Frazzle me for a deck-swab if I don't b'lieve that's the *Toreador*," exclaimed Tom Dollar. "Ye figgered right, Cap'n, what the Portygee 'ud do. That must be her. She's run into a calm streak an' we've overhauled her."

"It's her all right," confirmed Cap'n Pepper, coming on the poop after a look aloft, his eyes glinting. "I'll likely be alongside of her by crack o' dawn tomorrow."

To his infinite disgust, shortly after midnight the wind died out. The long Gulf swells, sweeping with oily smoothness against the low black sides of the brigantine, kept lifting her and then settling her down into an inky hollow, which motion produced a thundering slat from her enormous fore and aft mainsail and necessitated lowering the sail.

Candage had gone below in the latter part of the first watch but, finding it impossible to sleep on account of the stifling heat in the cabin, he finally sprang in disgust from his bunk and joined the captain on the poop. A heavy mist was creeping across the water from inshore; even at that distance it bore the dank, sickly smell of rank vegetation, and fetid fruit. Huge cumulus clouds were also coming up from the westward to meet it, and soon every star was blotted out and the ship was shrouded in blackness.

It was while they were waiting for a breeze that Cap'n Pepper deemed the time opportune for partially enlightening the navy man concerning the object of this cruise.

"Listen!" he broke off suddenly, laying his hand on the navy man's arm. "Do you hear anythin'?"

"I heard a noise like the slattin' o' sails," announced Tom Dollar, who had nearly run over them on his way to the binnacle. "Thar' 'tis again. Wear me under bare poles if that ain't a schooner's rags a-slattin' somewhere off'n our port beam."

"It's the Portygee!" whispered the Sea Fox jubilantly. "Pass the word along to the men, Mr. Dollar, not to show no kind of a light an' not to make no noise. We'll likely get a crack at that feller in the mornin'. There's a four-knot current sweepin' from Cape Palmas east'ard an' both vessels are in it.

"We'll have wind and plenty of it before the regular land breeze sets in," declared Candage, as large drops of rain began spattering the deck. "A squall will follow this rain. I hope it won't separate us from the schooner. I wouldn't miss this fight. Captain, for a farm down East."

Conversation was cut short by a terrific downpour of rain, during which they sheltered themselves under the drooping folds of the mainsail. Then came a fierce squall which lasted not more than five minutes, subsiding into a gentle westerly.

"I hope the wind don't hold in this quarter," grumbled Cap'n

Pepper, slatting the water from his sou'wester. "If it does it means chasing the *Toreador* on a wind, an' I've an idea she's faster on that point than the *Wild Pigeon*."

To his delight, in a few minutes the wind hauled to the southward. All plain sail was made and the ship put on a course half a point to windward of the one Cap'n Pepper knew the *Toreador* must take to get clear of the stiff current. The *Wild Pigeon* now had the wind a point abaft the starboard beam, and there was not a vessel on the coast could touch her when she was running free.

Not for nothing had Cap'n Pepper been termed the Sea Fox; the breaking dawn disclosed the Portuguese craft a point on the lee bow and about two miles distant. Whereupon the arms chest was at once looted of its weapons—carbines, pistols, and cutlasses. Ammunition was put in readiness, the gun sponged and reloaded, matches placed handy, and the decks sanded to keep them from becoming slippery with blood.

Mr. Candage looked on these preparations with an approving eye. It was plainly evident that the Sea Fox was no amateur at this mode of fighting.

Inshore about three miles distant, like a great gray wall, was the fog. This fog was dangerous in that anything might come out of it; perhaps that slavers' dread, a cruiser.

THE GREAT snowy sails of the schooner *Toreador* flashed in the bright sunlight. The long black hull with its graceful streamlines glided through the water with just a touch of foamy ripple at her bows, making all of nine knots in that moderate breeze.

The Sea Fox paced the poop of his vessel with Candage and Tom Dollar, every now and then taking the bearings of the chase, from the compass, and looking up speculatively at her own towering spars that were carrying every rag she had on her.

"We're overhaulin' him slowly," he remarked after another squint into the binnacle. "We'll soon see whether he intends to run or show his teeth. Look at that, will ye! Don't that just beat hell!" he exclaimed a moment later as the schooner suddenly flattened in her sheets and went reaching along close-hauled on the starboard tack. "He knows that I can't head as close-to the wind as him but he prob'ly figgers that I'll try to follow him just the same. He's got another think a-comin'. He can't hold long on that course or he'll be back again in the current. Meanwhile I'll try a trick or two myself."

The lee stuns'ls were taken in and Cap'n Pepper braced up the yards and hauled his wind so that it was only a point free. He held this course for a half-hour, by which time the *Toreador* was a mile on his weather beam. Then he took in the remaining stuns'ls, braced sharp up, got good headway on her and went about.

"I'll keep tackin' till I either drive him back to the coast or force him to fight," he explained. "Ah! Taveira's got it through his thick head at last what I'm up to. Here he comes."

The *Toreador* was sweeping round in a graceful curve and in another minute was heading directly for the *Wild Pigeon*. At the same time the Portuguese colors flew to her main truck with the American flag upside down underneath. No greater insult was ever given by one captain to another, signifying as it did that the flag underneath was fit only for a door-mat.

The navy man's eyes flashed.

"What wouldn't I give to be able to fire a broadside from the *Porpoise* into him now," he grated. His eyes rested longingly on the twelve-pounder on the poop. "When he gets within range, Captain, do let me have a shot at him with that," he entreated.

The captain nodded assent and Candage, with the aid of some of the husky crew, swung the 2,300-pound gun into position.

When Candage, who knew to a hair the range of the gun he was handling, judged the schooner was close enough he carefully sighted the gun and then stepped back as Tom Dollar kissed the touch-hole with a lighted match. The big gun belched and thundered and when the smoke cleared away the crew burst into a rousing cheer. The fore topmast of the schooner was shot clean away and was now dangling over the port fore chains.

Still the *Toreador* held her course, while her fore rigging became suddenly alive with men clearing the tangled mess and cutting the wreckage adrift. The falling topmast must have put her Long Tom out of commission, for she made no attempt to use it and probably did not care to lose her advantageous position by yawing to fire a broadside.

"Stand by your sheets and braces, men," commanded the Sea Fox, watching the approaching schooner coolly; "an' work lively when ye get the word."

When the two vessels were about a cable's length apart, the wheel of the *Wild Pigeon* was jammed hard down and she went in stays. As she spun on the other tack the positions of the ships were reversed. The speed of the schooner carried her on just right for the brigantine to range by her stern, and Tom Dollar improved the opportunity by raking her decks and doing terrible execution with the pivot-gun forward, double-shotted with grape. The next moment the *Wild Pigeon* was rounding to under the schooner's counter and the grappling-irons flew and held.

"Never in my life did I see prettier work," exulted Candage. "It couldn't have been done better in the navy."

"Go after 'em, men!" shouted Cap'n Pepper, and his crew, armed with cutlass and pistol, swarmed over the rail.

The Sea Fox with Candage and Tom Dollar bounded on her poop rail and from there to her deck. The latter had hardly felt the planks under his feet before he had discharged his pistol into the face of the schooner's mate and thus one of her officers was accounted for in a twinkling.

A swarthy, squat, gorilla-looking man with one eye and an enormous lump on his back came bounding like an ape across the top of the house, bellowing in Portuguese for his men to butcher and give no quarter. It was Taveira. He made a swipe, a slashing cut with his heavy cutlass at Cap'n Pepper, which the latter avoided by leaping back nimbly. Before the infuriated Portuguese could renew the attack Candage brought his cutlass down on Taveira's misshapen skull; he dropped like a poled ox.

"Why didn't you leave him to me?" growled the Sea Fox. "He was my meat by right."

"They all look alike to me," yelled back Candage, his eyes glowing like hot steel with the lust of battle.

Even with their leaders gone the crew of the *Toreador* continued fighting with all the brutal ferocity of wild beasts defending their lair. But, just as the issue of the battle seemed trembling in the balance, suddenly the gratings on the main hatch burst upward and a gigantic Negro Robin Hood, the *Wild Pigeon's* bosun—with twenty savage Gold Coast natives that he had liberated, streamed over the hatch-coamings. They all wielded five-foot lengths of firewood of tough African oak and at once, with horrible yells, they started mowing a swathe through the Portuguese.

This was more than the battered remainder of the schooner's crew had bargained for, and after a last feeble stand they were all driven below into the fo'c's'le and the scuttle fastened over them. The fight had lasted just twenty-seven minutes, during which time eighteen of the Portuguese and eleven of the boarders had been killed.

"Hoo-roo for Tippecanoe an' Tyler too," yelled Tom Dollar, when he saw the battle was won. "Hoo-roo ag'in."

"Good enough, Mr. Dollar," conceded Cap'n Pepper, tearing off a piece of his shirt sleeve and holding it to a bleeding cut on his left eyebrow, "but we'll celebrate when we get clear of this mess. Clear the decks so's ye can work, an' then get the slaves aboard the *Wild Pigeon* as quick's ye can. We can't tell what minute a cruiser might come nosin' round."

"Hold on there, Captain Pepper," broke in Candage. "You seem to forget that I'm a representative of the United States Government and as such is my duty to declare the *Toreador* and her cargo a lawful prize of that country. I will see, however, that the part you've all taken in capturing her will be fully reported to the Secretary of the Navy. Now I'll—"

"Belay that palaver, Mr. Candage," snapped the Sea Fox, who

was in no mood to brook interference at this critical moment. "I'll turn the schooner over to ye just as soon's I can. I know you'd be pained at the sight of what I'm a-goin' to do, so I'll put ye in the dog-house* for a little while. I'll let ye out the minnit we're through our business an' then ye can have your hooker. Robin Hood, show this gentleman to the dog-house."

"Yes sah," grinned the giant bosun. "Jus' come this way ef yah please, sah."

Candage well knew the futility of protesting further. "Pity you can't keep a good clearance when you have it, Captain," he concluded. "Once you put slaves aboard of your vessel I shall have to condemn her also."

Cap'n Pepper chuckled and turned away. The navy man was put into the dog-house, the sliding door shut and securely fastened with a belaying pin wedged in the back of it.

THE TRANSFER of the slaves took some little time. But finally, when the Sea Fox had his original two hundred and five slaves and sixty more besides, the warning cry of the lookout stationed at the masthead rang out.

"Sail—ho. Dead on the weather beam."

As the Sea Fox had more than half feared, a cruiser flying the American colors at her peak had emerged from the fog and was now bearing down on them under a press of canvas. She was the brig-of-war *Perry,* now about a mile distant.

Instantly Cap'n Pepper withdrew his crew from the schooner, grappling-ropes were cut, and slowly the vessels began drifting apart as the *Wild Pigeon* filled her head sails.

There was perhaps thirty-feet separating them when Tom Dollar uttered a startled oath and drew the captain's attention to the schooner's poop. Taveira, who had been forgotten in the heat of battle and left for dead, was now seen slowly getting on his feet. He clambered painfully onto the main sheerpole, took

* Officers quarters on deck when the cabin is given over to female slaves.—J.K.W.

one look at the approaching war vessel and, like a monstrous crab, scuttled below into the cabin.

"He's a-goin' to blow the schooner up, I do b'lieve!" gasped Tom Dollar. "Ye know he swears no cruser'll take him alive. Damnation! I thought that hellion was outa the reck'nin' for good. I—" he broke off suddenly while his tanned features assumed an ashy-gray color. "By God!" he jerked out. "I left that poor officer cooped up in the dog-house. An'—an' I promised to let him out when I was through. I clean forgot him."

The next moment there was a splash in the water and the Sea Fox was tearing through the sea in the direction of the schooner. He was not more than two minutes reaching her chains. Climbing up, he swung onto her deck and made for the dog-house door. Kicking out the belaying pin, he slid the door back.

"Jump overboard quick'n hell before you're blowed up!" he yelled to Candage and dashed for the cabin.

At the foot of the companionway his ear-drums vibrated from the sudden report of a pistol fired in close quarters.

"Someone has shot himself," said the voice of Candage at his elbow.

Cap'n Pepper gave a snarl of dispair.

"You fool, why didn't ye save yourself!" he threw over his shoulder as he ran into the captain's room.

Taveira lay sprawled on the carpet-rug, the smoking pistol gripped tightly in his stiffening fingers. The *sput-sput* of a burning fuse could be plainly heard. Lifting the top of the desk, they saw a round hole in one corner smudged with smoke.

"It's already in the hold!" flashed Cap'n Pepper. "Jump over the side quick, you. There ain't no use both of us gettin' killed."

Quickly he rolled the body away and tossed up the rug, disclosing a small hatch. A second sufficed to throw this aside and Cap'n Pepper was squeezing down through the square aperture. In the darkness of the hold he made out the red end of the fuse sputtering over the chines of a cask. Sweating and swearing, the Sea Fox worked his way to it and gave a jerk; it came away in his hands to the length of three fathoms.

He rubbed it out against the bilge of a cask and, coming back to the hatch, handed it up to Candage, who was still standing waiting.

"You've saved those two hundred or more slaves still remaining in the hold," declared the naval officer as the Sea Fox climbed out of the hatchway and stood for a moment dashing the sweat from his eyes. "You may be a slaver and all that, but, by gad, I'm proud to know you." He seized the captain's hand and shook it heartily.

"I ain't got no time to palaver now," blurted Cap'n Pepper, making like a flash for the deck.

Here he cast a hasty glance about and saw that the brig-of-war was within pistol shot.

"The game is up, Captain," announced Candage. "Wish it was someone else I had to take though. Makes it bad you having those slaves aboard, but I'll do all I can for you. You can trust me. I'm Commodore Gregory, you know."

THE NEXT moment it was plainly apparent that the Sea Fox had no intention of trusting the commodore or any one else wearing a naval uniform. Placing a hand on the rail, he vaulted overboard. Four minutes later his dripping figure could be discerned standing on the poop of his vessel.

Meanwhile the commodore had leaped into the main rigging and with a handkerchief was wigwagging a message to the *Perry*. Whereupon she immediately maneuvered so as to glide in between the schooner and the brigantine. The latter was fairly trapped. The breeze had stiffened but if the Sea Fox had attempted to beat to windward he undoubtedly would have had his masts shot away for his trouble.

"Ain't it just plumb hell?" inquired Tom Dollar of nobody in particular. "All this here work for nothin'. It won't be bail for me this time nuther. I skipped it twice already. Waal, we had a tarnation fine scrap an' no mistake, so hoo-roo an' be damned to 'em."

"Shut up, you!" snapped the Sea Fox. "So long's we got planks under our feet we got a chance an' I'm a-goin' to take it. That cruiser won't try to hull us for fear of killing the slaves. He'll try for our masts an' riggin'. Stand by your braces, Mr. Dollar, ready to square in lively. Leave one man here at the main sheet. It's goin' to be some squeak, for I ain't got room to clear the *Perry*, but as long's we can swing a rope-yarn we'll keep a-goin'."

He then hauled down his flag in token of surrender and took the wheel. Spinning it hard up, he kept off and nodded his head to Tom Dollar. The fore yards swung quietly. The very boldness of the Sea Fox's plan made for its success. Never, against such overwhelming odds, did the *Perry's* officers dream of his attempting to escape. They naturally supposed that the Sea Fox was about to heave-to close to them. To their unbounded astonishment and before they had realized what he was up to, he had swung by their stern so closely that he snapped off the *Perry's* spanker boom at the sheet-band like a pipestem.

Then, hauling his wind, he put the schooner between his vessel and the cruiser and, thus having rendered her guns unavailable, the Sea Fox piled the stuns'ls onto the *Wild Pigeon* and went skimming to the westward like a freed bird. Gone.

Commodore Gregory grinned and shouted an order to the *Perry's* officers. With wide eyes they were lining her pooprail within thirty feet of where he stood on the schooner. In another moment the brisk breeze bore to the ears of the fleeing brigantine's crew the sounds of three rousing cheers from at least eighty lusty throats.

"D'yer hear that now, Mr. Dollar?" exclaimed Cap'n Pepper. "They're cheerin' the commodore for capturin' the *Toreador*. Good luck to him, an' he's welcome to what we done toward it. He's a most likeable cuss an' a first-class fightin' man. Ye seen that today, an', as sure's your name's Tom Dollar, if he hadn't been the gentleman he is we'd both be prisoners now aboard the *Perry*.

"He could 'a' got me by simply puttin' on that hatch just before I handed him the fuse. I could see in his eyes that he'd thought about that same thing, but he was too square to do it. I tell ye, Tom Dollar, that when Uncle Sam begins sendin' out them kinda men to the coast it's about time the Sea Fox was a-lookin' for his hole."

CRACKING THE BLACK JOKE

Wiley was the Sea Fox, as the men-o'-war patroling the West African coast could dolefully testify; but it remained for a British captain to discover a sense of humor in the American slaver—humor exhibited while capture and death frowned from the British guns above him.

"**HEIGH! HEIGH!** Go 'way, nigger. Why you palaver me, eh? You no sabbe me? Me Boollam Bill, de bes' pilot on dis Wes' Coast Afriky; yessa, me bes' pilot on dis yah Calabar Ribber. Me got big news for Gappen Pepper, de Sea Fox. Bimeby de *Black Joke* get you too much. Let go me now or I make noise like de tunder."

The hand of Robin Hood the herculean colored American bosun of the slaver brigantine *Wild Pigeon,* tightened on the breast of the long-tailed blue coat of the speaker, who had bounded over the rail from a canoe the moment before and, with a look of haughty contempt on his coal-black features, had attempted to push by the bosun on duty at the gangway.

"What for you no answer me when I asked your bus'ness?" growled the wrathful bosun. "Nobody done allowed 'board dis ship till dey gives de exact an' entire info'mation what dey come for, savvy?"

Reaching down from his height of six feet seven, he gathered Boollam Bill up in his arms, made two strides along the deck and, whisking up the visitor's coat-tails, sat that important person's bare haunches firmly on the shining brass plate ornamenting the top of the amidship capstan, which under the fierce sun of an African noonday was nearly at a white heat.

At once Boollam Bill's thick lips assumed the shape and expansiveness of a motor tire and from the enormous cavity

27

burst a sound which rent the air with such a clamorous vigor as to startle the whole ship's company.

Under the awning on the poop the Sea Fox and his mate, Tom Dollar, were entertaining a distinguished visitor, no less a person than the Duke Ephraim, as the King of Duketown—Old Calabar—was called.

"De debbil!" ejaculated his fat highness, his tall white beaver hat, ornamented with a broad gold band, bounding from his head as his pendulous paunch rose in fright. "Who make'm fearful damn noise?"

By the time he had recovered his hat and steadied his nerves with a stiff drink of rum and lime juice from his tumbler, which nothing short of an explosion directly beneath his chair could have loosened from his hold, Boollam Bill came bounding up the poop ladder with the bosun giving him a shove in the rear.

"Heigh—heigh; He t'ink umself berry claber!" sputtered Boollam Bill. "Me no—"

"This sassy bush-nigger, Cappen, sah," broke in the bosun, "comes 'board contr'y to orders an' I disciperlin' him a bit, sah. He say he got berry important news. Sumpin' 'bout a black joke, sah."

"THE *BLACK JOKE!*" blurted Cap'n Pepper, half-rising from his seat, his piercing black eyes snapping wide open, his heavy jaw sagging; then, settling back in his chair, he threw a look of grave apprehension toward his mate.

The latter lifted his rangy form from the edge of the skylight, his prominent larynx racing up and down in his lean throat, revolting at the quid he had bolted in his sudden agitation upon hearing that dreaded name.

"Hell's lifts!" he choked out. "We ain't been anchored in the river three hours when here comes a whole fog o' trouble, looks like."

Boollam Bill, quite elated at the sensation he had created, drew himself up and threw out his chest.

"Me tell you 'bout de *Black Joke* too much, Cappen, s'pose you gimme plenty 'dash.' You sabbe me berry 'liable, Cappen."

Despite his anxiety the Sea Fox grinned. Bollam Bill was widely known as the most consummate rascal on the Coast, combining with the duty of pilot that of acting as spy for the cruisers and slavers and often duping both. Captains of traders also looked on him askance, one of them complaining that Bill

had once robbed him of everything about the decks but the hatch-coamings and the anchor.

It was this knowledge that restrained the Sea Fox from immediately demanding that Boollam Bill should disclose his tidings concerning H.M. Brig-of-war the *Black Joke*, a vessel the very name of which started a cold sweat on the faces of even the boldest and most resourceful of the slaver captains.

The Sea Fox deliberately placed one thick muscular leg over the other, hunched his stocky frame further back into his canvas deck-chair and surveyed Boollam Bill from under the brim of his palm-leaf hat with eyes as expressionless as two lumps of coal.

"Well!" he jerked out finally. "What's all this no good palaver ye got about that ole tub, the *Black Joke?* Spit it out an' make it short."

Whereupon Boollam Bill, though his sanguine expectations of a big present were somewhat diminished by the seeming indifference of the three listeners, rattled on glibly for fully ten minutes carefully descanting on every detail of his news. The sum and substance of his remarks was that while he was piloting a Liverpool trader from Mimbo to Jamestown he had counted three British and two American cruisers well in-shore, and when off Tom Shot bank, just before crossing Calabar bar, they had been boarded by the captain of the *Black Joke*, Sir Harry Clavering himself, who had questioned Bill closely concerning the movements of slavers in the Bonny and Calabar Rivers.

"He ask me berry 'tic'ler 'bout you, Cappen Peper," finished Boollam Bill, his splendid teeth flashing in a wide smile. "He say he hear you berry claber an' he want to see you too much."

"Which means," rasped the Sea Fox, springing up, the nostrils of his short freckled nose expanding angrily, "what ye could 'a' said in lessen a dozen words: the *Black Joke* is here to get us. What time was it when Sir Harry boarded you, can ye tell me that?"

"I tink 'bout eight de clock, Cappen, dis morning."

"H-mm! good thing I didn't wait till daylight to cross the bar; he might 'a' saw us comin' in. It's evident he don't know we're here yet. Looks like we got to run the blockade of all them cruisers goin' out, Mr. Dollar."

"Damn! Too much man-of-wars!" grumbled Duke Ephraim. "Whaffor they come to my country?"

Greatly vexed at the idea of this interference with his lucrative commerce in human flesh, the king refilled his glass entirely with rum, disdaining the lime-juice bottle proffered by his Uwei slave.

"Whaffor they name dat brig-of-war the *Black Joke*?" he asked, after gulping half the fiery potion in two swallows. "I hear plenty talk long time but no see her. She nebber come Calabar before."

"A Britisher's idee o' bein' funny," snapped the Sea Fox. "She used to be the slaver *Henri Quatre* an' when she was capt'ered they fitted her out as a cruiser and afterward named her the *Black*

Joke she was so tarnation successful in seizin' other slavers. She sails like a streak o' light an' she's become a reg'lar terror to them Congo slavers sence Sir Harry took her. What got into his head to come up here? Shouldn't wonder if Commodore Gregory had a hand in it somehow."

"Hell's lifts!" chimed in Tom Dollar. "Ye can bet he never left the Congo on his own accord; he's too fond o' huntin' el'phants. He's killed more of 'em than any other man livin'. Writ a book 'bout it, I heerd."

"That may be, but his huntin' grain turns to sunthin' else besides el'phants," observed the Sea Fox, "remember, with the 'ception o' Gregory, he's capt'ered more prizes than all the rest o' them Johnny Wars put together. But all this talk ain't gettin' us nowhere," he added passionately, kicking off his old leather slippers and feeling the deck with bare, tanned feet, as if he would communicate his troubles to his beloved ship. "We gotta have action, *action!* D'yer hear. I'll start with ye right now, Boollam Bill."

"You gimme plenty dash," purred the latter.

"To be sure. Mr. Dollar, take Bill below an' give him anythin' his heart desires, after he has a drink o' R. an' L. (rum and laudanum) that is." He put his mouth to the mate's ear and added: "We gotta keep him under the lee o' our pistols till we get out o' this mess. Cain't take no chances on him, understan'?"

The mate nodded and the unsuspecting pilot was led away.

FANNED BY his assiduous slave, Duke Ephraim had subsided into a gentle snooze. Observing this the Sea Fox went to the rail and stood looking over the river which, full of decayed animal and vegetable matter, was the color of burned soup. He looked absently at Duketown, that conglomeration of thatched mud-brick houses, conspicuous among which was the immense palaver house and Duke Ephraim's "English house" or palace. The town lay baking under the blazing sun and enveloped in a quivering haze arising from the mudflats along the river front.

From this uninviting sight the slaver switched his gaze to

the motley array of canoes bobbing at the landings, and from them to the shipping at anchor. There were two English trading-brigs and a battered old New Bedford whaler whose captain had come in to trade off the remains of his slop-chest before proceeding home.

A gleam of interest flickered in the Sea Fox's eyes as they rested on the whaleship. The next moment, keeping pace with the idea growing in his mind, he noted every detail of her ensemble—the carved rope with tarnished flakey patches of gilding on it, surrounding her name, *Martha Crabtree;* the blistered, grayish-black paint on her hull; the frayed, bleached running-gear, hanging slovenly in a bight from the fairleaders; the four beautiful boats at her clumsy wooden davits; and the large cutting-in stage hoisted perpendicularly outside of the starboard bulwarks forward of the gangway.

Presently a broad grin spread over his rugged features and facing suddenly inboard he slammed a fist into the open palm of his right hand.

"By the devil's great tail-block, I b'lieve I gotta good scheme," he exulted. "Sir Harry ain't huntin' el'phants now, he'll find out. Well, how's Boollam Bill?" this to Tom Dollar, who at that moment came on the poop.

"Sleepin' peaceful as a babe, in the doghouse, an' leg-irons on," replied the mate.

"Good. If I'd 'a' let him go he'd been aboard the *Black Joke* afore mornin' sell-in' his information 'bout me for another dash. I know the critter. Ah! I see the Duke's come to life ag'in. Must be thirsty."

Cap'n Pepper himself helped his majesty to another drink.

"Duke, today is Saturday, the thirtieth of November," he said. "The Harmattan wind'ull begin to blow in a day or two an' I wanta take advantage of it. Now listen careful, Duke, I gotta have four hundred-sixty slaves ready in your barracoons by Wednesday night. Can ye do it?"

"What 'bout de *Black Joke* outside de bar?" asked Duke Ephraim.

"T'hell with him. Can ye furnish the slaves."

"Me get'm two days mebbe."

"Not the kind I want, you won't. No sick or *tick-tick* niggers for me, ye know. Say Wednesday night, Duke, an' over an' above their price I'll throw in a ten-gallon kag of the fines' ole Medford ye ever smacked yer lips over."

Duke Ephraim's eyes glistened. He ran the tip of his tongue tentatively over his lower lip and got slowly to his feet.

"Berry good. Me have dem den, Cappen," he agreed, and, rising slowly to his feet, he extended his hand and gave the slaver the grip of the Egbo, a powerful native secret order, of which Duke Ephraim was the head. The Sea Fox was one of the few white men admitted to this order and held the highest degree attainable to any not of the blood-royal. It entitled the possessor to the privilege of sitting in council at the palaver house and, what was of far more importance to the Sea Fox, the help and protection of the Duke and all the powerful chiefs of the country.

With the potent aid of this order he was able to accomplish, in the short space of four days, what would otherwise have taken him a month and then only under the most favorable circumstances.

"Get the dingy alon'side the gangway with a couple o' men in it, Mr. Dollar," ordered Cap'n Pepper when presently the royal visitor departed shoreward in his six-oared gig. "I got sunthin' a-stewin' in my mind an' I'm goin' over an' dicker with the skipper of that blubber-hunter. Shouldn't wonder if he'd like to make a little money on the side."

Going below to his cabin, he took a small bag of gold from the safe, crammed it into his pocket and, coming on deck, dropped into the stern of the dingy and was pulled over to the *Martha Crabtree*. He returned to his ship in less than an hour and the mate, observing on his tanned face the smile of a man who has completed a fine stroke of business, flashed an inquiring look.

"Ever been a-whalin', Tom Dollar?" asked the Sea Fox.

The mate gave a snort of disgust.

"Hell's lifts, no! None o' them stinkin' grease-tubs for me, Cap'n."

"Too bad. If ye had ye mighta been a great help. Me an' Cap'n Blackmer, the skipper o' the *Crabtree*, is a-goin' to turn this hooker into a whaler." Seeing the mate's look of astonishment, he added, "I'll explain later; it's cost me a pretty penny, I can tell ye that now, an' we gotta shake a leg. The tide's beginning to turn so man the windlass an' get up yer anchor. The whaler an' us is goin' up the river a few miles out o' sight an' begin operations. They ain't no use denyin' the fact that we're in the tightest hole we ever got into sence we been in the bus'ness; them cruisers has us corked up tight's a bee in a bottle. The *Black Joke*, howsomever, is the one I'm a-feared on."

He glanced over the decks of his splendid craft and sighed.

"I know we're boun' to be capt'ered some time, but I allus hoped it would be an American that done it. Anyway, we got the Harmattan wind to help us when we go, Tom Dollar, an' we'll try an' crack the *Black Joke* with a red one, the red fog."

THE *WILD PIGEON* and the whaleship were moored in the little creek below Creektown by 4:30 that afternoon and the captain of the whaler immediately placed his crew aboard the slaver and began the work of transformation. Duke Ephraim also provided a gang of men to clean her copper and to give her shining black hull a weather-worn appearance by abrading the paint with pieces of grindstone. Three of the whaler's spare boats, fully equipped for the business of whaling, were swung to regulation wooden davits, two boats on the port and one on the starboard side abreast of the forerigging. Lookout-rings were placed at the mastheads and the slaver's extremely long yards, which in themselves were sufficient to awaken suspicion in the alert mind of Sir Harry, were camouflaged to appear shorter by shifting the lifts and braces inboard a little and then painting the outside yard-ends a light color.

The sails, of the best canvas and cut to fit as flat as a board, were systematically dirtied and patched with old canvas; patch upon patch after the manner of whalers. Her six guns were shored up just abaft the fore hatches and, concealed with a tarpaulin cover, looked for all the world like the regular try-works. Even the false deck of light boards, which protects a whaler's permanent decks from the razor-edged spades when cutting up blubber, was laid and two boat-steerers went round gashing it lightly with spades. After it had been plentifully swabbed with whale-oil one would have sworn that innumerable blanket pieces of blubber had been cut up on that deck. Lastly the brigantine's beautiful clipper bows were framed and boarded over so that she presented the apple-bows typical of a whaler. This false work, being nearly all above water, did not impair her speed qualities.

In fact by Wednesday morning the *Wild Pigeon*, to all appearances, was a whaler in every detail save one. This, the Sea Fox, who spent the most of the time ashore selecting his slaves as fast as the Duke's agents brought them in, noticed as soon as he came aboard that morning.

"Why didn't ye give me a stage the same's ye got aboard yer vessel?" he demanded, pointing to the cutting-in stage on the *Crabtree*.

Captain Blackmer explained that a permanent stage was not absolutely necessary as many small whalers merely slung side stages when about to cut in a whale.

"Never mind if they do," persisted Cap'n Pepper. "I wanta stage jest where ye got yours. An' make it a couple o' feet longer than usual so's it 'ull loom up like the frame of a barn. The men I'm goin' up against notice everythin'; in fac', Cap'n, if I hadn't allus been partic'ler 'bout little things that don't seem o' no account at the time, they'd 'a' put me out o' business long ago."

And so the stage, which was to figure so prominently later on, was in its place by nightfall.

Just after dark the two vessels got smoothly under way and dropped down the river. At Duketown the *Wild Pigeon,* the name on her stern now reading *John Williams,* anchored and began taking her slaves aboard from Duke Ephraim's large canoes. The whaler kept on her way for the anchorage opposite Herald Point, where she was to wait for the slaver. At daylight, or as soon as the Harmattan wind set in, they would cross the bar together; thus presenting the appearance, should they meet the eagle eye of a cruiser's lookout, of two old whalers cruising together.

About midnight the slaver joined her consort and hardly had her anchor plunged into the sullen water when trouble, swift and overwhelming, struck the Sea Fox. Robin Hood reported that Boollam Bill had made good his escape.

In some manner, not yet ascertained, he had broken his shackles and gone. Just when, the bosun didn't know, but it must have been sometime after six o'clock, for at that time Robin Hood himself had taken his supper to him in the dog-house, as the officers' deck quarters were called. The bosun surmised that Bill had flitted either when they were all busy getting under way or were taking on the slaves.

Thunderstruck at this news, Cap'n Pepper stared through the starlight at the faintly distinguishable features of his old mate.

"That's what I get for tryin' to help anybody!" he groaned. "I was a-goin' to pervide a good home for Boollam Bill on one o' Faversham's plantations. He would 'a' fetched six hundred dollars or more. An' now—"

He was interrupted by the arrival of one of Duke Ephraim's spies with more bad news. The Brazilian schooner *Ou Voador* whose captain had been drinking to the point of recklessness, had come down from up-river that afternoon and, disregarding all warning, had loaded up with slaves the Sea Fox had rejected for some slight blemish or other. Crossing the bar at sundown, he had made a dash for the open sea.

Twenty minutes later the schooner had been snapped up by

the *Black Joke* and was now on her way, under a prize-crew, to Sierra Leone for adjudication.

"Hurroo!" barked Tom Dollar. "Them Johnny Wars is right on the job an' no mistake. Devil take me ef I wouldn't be as tickled as a mermaid with a new tail ef I was back home in Lewes, Delaware, right now. Bet ye a plug o' the best that Boollam Bill is aboard one o' them cruisers a-tellin' 'em all about it by the time we get outside."

"That depends," returned the Sea Fox. "If the damn cuss left us in Creektown, as he did prob'ly, he won't make it over the bar any sooner'n we do. Ye forget he's got to dodge all them canoes the Duke's got policin' the river till I get out."

Forthwith he dispatched the native spy for Captain Blackmer and upon the latter's arrival apprised him of the situation.

"Tain't no use turnin' back," continued the Sea Fox. "Them Johnny Wars is here to stay, looks like, an' we gotta run the blockade sooner or later, so I'm a-goin' out. Go aboard, Cap'n, an' stan' by. The Duke's man here 'ull go with ye an' pilot ye out, an' I'll foller close behind. Mebbe if they do see us they won't pay no 'tention to two old whalers pluggin' along. But be ready as soon's the Harmattan begins to blow. That wind brings the red fog an' that's my best bet now."

It was indeed. That meteorological freak of the West Coast, beginning on or about the first of December and continuing until the middle of March, the Harmattan. This wind commences at a little before sunrise and dies out about noon. It is burdened with a red dust so thick that objects are discernible only at a short distance, especially near the coast.

Presently Captain Blackmer, accompanied by the spy, returned to his ship, leaving the Sea Fox and his two officers pacing the poop of the slaver every cell in their brains aching with anxiety, every nerve jumping at the sudden mysterious noises of an African night—the faint, agonized blat of a goat on a far hillside as a leopard's fangs met in his throat; the bark of a baboon; the acute cries of the flying-foxes wrangling over some fruit; and now and then the whip-like reports of the ripe pods on a self-fire tree exploding from atmospheric causes. Not a breath of wind stirred the broad surface of the river, reflecting myriads of great stars.

A little before dawn the loosed sails, hanging in their gear from the yards, rustled; the great mainsail, already hoisted, partly filled and, dragging the heavy boom over to starboard, brought up on the sheet. A cold, dry wind from the east-northeast fanned the cheeks of the Sea Fox and his officers. It was the beginning of the Harmattan.

AN HOUR later, shortly after sunrise, under all plain sail, the whaler and the slaver crossed Calabar Bar. Enveloped in a cloud of red dust so dense at times that the Sea Fox could barely make out the huge proportions of Robin Hood on lookout on the fo'c's'le head, the two vessels trimmed yards on the starboard tack and, with a six-knot breeze off the quarter, laid a west by south course to run out of the Bight of Biafra.

The vessels were now running parallel to each other about a cable's length apart, the slaver gradually forging past the other.

"Hard down yuh wheel—hard down!" there came a sudden roar from Robin Hood. "Vessel right ahead, sah!"

The wheel spun and, as the slaver thundered up into the wind, her Britannic Majesty's steamer *Firefly* loomed out of the red mist, her squat bulk not a biscuit toss away.

"What ship is that?" bellowed an apoplectic lieutenant from her bridge.

The *John Williams* o' New Bedford, United States of Ameriky!" responded the Sea Fox.

"Well, what the blue blazes do you mean messing about here with all your dirty rags on in this fog? Your old grease-tub will be foul of one of our cruisers if you don't watch out!"

"An' what do *you* mean," exploded the incensed Tom Dollar, "a-takin' up the hull ocean with that steam wash-b'iler o' yourn? You'll skeer all the whales in creation. I've a good mind to report ye to Queen Victorie!"

The naval officer had not quite finished his profane peroration on whalers in general and this one in particular when, as the slaver braced her yards and disappeared in the fog, he was forced to give his undivided attention to the *Martha Crabtree,* which just then came lumbering along.

"Ye hadn't oughta riled that gold-boun' feller that way, Tom Dollar," chuckled Cap'n Pepper. "But," he added gleefully, "ye can see our disguise is jest the proper thing. He never s'pected nothin'. I'll bet that officer 'ud be a tarnation sight madder than he is now if he l'arned that he let the Sea Fox get by with four-hundred-sixty slaves aboard. Anyway, we're safe now. Ye can see Boollam Bill ain't had a chance to betray us yet."

The mate shook his head.

"We ain't outa the woods yet by no manner o' means, Cap'n," he announced dubiously. "Thar', hell's lifts, what'd I tell ye? Listen! Thar's a Johnny War right close aboard of us a-keepin' his lead goin'."

"A quarter less twelve—by the deep twelve—an' a half twelve," came the droning chant, uncannily near, of a leadsman in the main-chains of a cruiser.

Fog is very deceptive conveyer of sound and to the two slavers, straining eyes and ears at the low poop-rail, the voice appeared to be off their starboard quarter when in reality it was directly astern.

"I can't see nothin'," complained the mate. "Wish we had eyes like Robin Hood there forrad, we might—"

Crash! Tom Dollar nearly bit his tongue in two as at that instant the port cathead of the man-of-war ripped off a piece of the starboard molding on the slaver's stern. The impact precipitated the Sea Fox head first into the green sea and his mate would have assuredly accompanied him but for the fact that the officer was holding onto the main topmast backstay at the time.

The Sea Fox cleaved the water to a considerable depth and was swept a little distance from his ship by the current before he could right himself and make for the surface. As he was coming up a heavy, chunky object plumped onto his left shoulder and a small line scraped his ear. Throwing up his hand, he grasped the small wooden handhold of a headline and broke water just as the leadsman, who had kept to his duty despite the collision, was excitedly making his report to the officer of the deck.

"A quarter less two, sir, an' my line fouled on somethin,' sir," he explained, amazed.

The officer was more startled at this abrupt shoaling of the water than he had been at grazing another vessel, and he was roaring out the order to tack ship when the glistening bald pate of the Sea Fox appeared over the top of the hammock rail.

"It's all right!" shouted the slaver, leaping lightly to the deck and addressing the captain, a well knit, kindly-looking man with an immense blond beard. "This here leadsman took soundin's off'n me. Ye ain't shoalin' yer water none an' ye can hold yer course."

He blinked about, his practised eyes taking in his surroundings at a glance—the grinning crew in the clean white uniform of the British navy; the four long guns on each side which, with two bow-chasers and a big pivot gun amidships, formed her battery; the towering spars piercing the red haze; the immense length of her lower yards.

An apprehensive shiver went over him as he looked at those yards. No regular man-of-war brig ever carried yards like these. Surely Fate could not have played him such a dirty trick as to throw him aboard the very vessel he dreaded above all others!

His troubled eyes roved aft, seeking something to disabuse his mind of the suspicion rapidly taking root there. As a group of men moved away from the front of the poop to execute some order, they exposed its glaring white surface. Painted there in letters so vividly black and large that they seemed to leap out at him was the name. The *Black Joke*.

"WHEN I see that name, Tom Dollar, derned if my laigs didn't seem to buckle like a t'gallant-mast in a squall," declared the Sea Fox, half an hour later on his own poop.

The red fog providentially lifting a moment or two after he had pitched overboard, the mate had seen him climbing up the side of the cruiser and had promptly dispatched the dingy for him.

"Yesser, I've jest put in the oneasiest an' at the same time the pleasantest fifteen minutes I ever see. That Sir Harry's a thor'bred an', when nobody didn't seem to recognize me, I really enjoyed talkin' to him. Soon's he found how matters stood an' that I was the skipper o' a whaler, he give a squint over at this hooker an' then took me down into his cabin. Sech a sight ye never saw; the man's plumb crazy 'bout huntin'. There was tiger skins an' el'phant tusks, an' stuffed birds everywhere ye looked. An' he showed me pic'ters in a book he's wrote 'bout it.

"Then he give me a drink an' was terrible eager to hear all 'bout whalin'. Haw-haw! You should 'a' seen his eyes flare like a puff o' blue smoke when I reeled off a couple o' twisters Cap'n Blackmer had told me. When I started to go, he said he'd be just tickled to death to come aboard here an' look 'round at our gear only he was afraid the fog might shut down a'gin any minute an' so he couldn't leave his ship. Mighty glad he couldn't too, I was. Well, as things stan's now, the joke is on the *Black Joke*, for fair, Tom Dollar. But we won't laugh very hearty till we get more blue water between us an' her guns."

" 'Twill be time enough then," agreed Tom Dollar. "We ain't so far off the coast but Boollam Bill still can turn a trick ef he tries hard 'nuff."

AT NOON the Harmattan subsided into a gentle two-knot zephyr and the red fog vanished, apparently sucked up by that terrible sun which turned the sky into an inverted bowl of glowing blue enamel. The five cruisers were lying in the shape of an elongated crescent, stretching seaward and about seven miles from tip to tip. In the center of this crescent was the *Black Joke*, about a musket shot to windward of the slaver and her consort which were jogging along about a half-cable's length apart. Both vessels had their lookouts aloft and were seemingly going about their business of whaling.

At three o'clock the position of the ships was much the same, with the exception of Sir Harry's vessel which had decreased her distance from the slaver by a good half.

It was a few minutes later that Tom Dollar and the bosun, coming up from the hold where they had been overseeing the loading of the slaves, were brought suddenly to an amazed standstill by the long drawn out cry of the lookouts at the whaler's mastheads.

"Ahhh, blo-o-ow; blo-o-ow! Ther-e-e she breaches! Ther-e-e she whitewaters!" came distinctly across the hundred yards of water intervening between the two vessels.

Tom Dollar straightened his lathlike frame to its full height, slammed his battered palm-leaf hat down on the deck and clutched convulsively at the opening in the neck of his red flannel undershirt.

"By great Nebbyc'anezzer's buck goat!" he exploded. "They're a-singin' out for whales. Don't that jest beat hell? If we'd been a gen'wine whaler we could 'a' cruised here till we grounded on our beef-bones an' never seed a spout. Now when we don't want the critters they're all ready to jump aboard. That's luck for ye, Robin Hood. What 'ull we do now," this to the Sea Fox, who came bounding up the companion way, a broad smile on his face.

"Do? I'm s'prised at ye, Tom Dollar, a-askin' that. Why we gotta carry this bluff out, o' course, so's not to excite s'picion."

"Aboard the *Williams!*" bellowed Cap'n Blackmer through his trumpet. "Small pod o' sparm whales 'bout a p'in on yer starboard bow an' 'bout a mile off. I'm goin' to run down an lower. Can't miss this chance."

"So be I!" yelled back the Sea Fox, his eyes dancing. "I paid two thousand dollars for this outfit," he confided to the mate, in answer to the latter's look of disgust, "an' it seems a shame not to use it once anyway."

Presently, while two boats were being made ready for lowering, the *Black Joke*, whose lookouts had apprised her captain of the whalers' evident designs, set her lower stu'nsails and, over-hauling the slaver, luffed up under her stern.

"Oh, Captain Marshall!" hailed Sir Harry, calling the Sea Fox by his alias. "May I go with you? It will be ripping sport."

"Glad to have ye," responded the Sea Fox affably. "Get ready an' I'll drop alongside an' get ye in a few minutes."

He turned to his grinning officers.

"Now, Mr. Dollar, as soon's we leave in the boats, ye an' Robin Hood go to the main masthead with yer glasses," he directed. "You keep watch o' us an' keep's close to us as ye can. Robin Hood you watch the cruisers. You've the sharpest eyes. If ye see them Johnny Wars beginnin' to signal sudden to one another, you'll know that Boollom Bill's been heard from an' it's time for ye to go. Don't waste a minnit but pile the kites to her an' show 'em how this old gal can pick up her feet when she's skeered. If ye can take us on 'thout losin' any advantage, do so; if ye can't, make for Sant Iago, Cuby, an' wait for us there. We'll follow in the *Crabtree*."

When within a short distance of the whales Cap'n Pepper, observing the *Crabtree* suddenly back her main-yard, did the same, lowering his two boats while the whaler dropped three.

Sir Harry, with the gray flannel shirt he had hastily donned rolled up to the elbows of his big white arms, was beaming down on the slaver captain as he steered his boat under the grim muzzles of the cruiser's gun to her gangway.

"I'm under your orders now, Captain, you know," said Sir Harry, dropping into the stern sheets; "but I'd consider it mighty good of you if you would let me harpoon a whale."

"Good thing I got some p'inters from Cap'n Blackmer," thought the slaver.

"Jest what I was a-figgerin' on, sir, an' so I left my harpooneer aboard," he said aloud. "Get into the bow an' stan' by. Yer irons is already bent onto the line. Shove off, men, an' up with the sail."

The wind increased and had shifted to the southwest, and was now bowling the boats steadily over a mass of leaping, flashing wavelets in the midst of which, a cable's length ahead, shot up the iridescent spouts of the leviathans. A flock of screaming whale-birds wheeled over the exposed surface of their glistening black bodies, swooping down every now and then to pick up the whale-lice clinging to the thick skin. A smell as of rotting seaweed suddenly greeted the nostrils of the hunters.

As they neared the pod an immense bull made a sudden breach, throwing his hundred and ten ton body nearly clear of the water, and coming down, caused the sea to boil up into a huge geyser.

Sir Harry, his blue eyes leaping with excitement, swung his blond beard around to face the Sea Fox.

"By jove! That fellow is larger than a whole herd of elephants," he exulted. "I really believe he could knock the ball off the truck of my ship's mainmast. Sorry I didn't bring my express rifle," he added.

Cap'n Pepper laughed.

"One o' them long nine-pounders o' yourn might wake him up a little, but a rifle bullet wouldn't rile him no more'n a b'iled pea. Stan' by now to give it to him; we'll be on in a minute."

AS THEY ran into the pod there came the *who-o-sh*, *who-o-sh* of the spouts all around them, but the Sea Fox steered steadily ahead, making for the bull. A half-minute more and the boat was sweeping close by the side of the leviathan. At Cap'n Pepper's command to "Give him hell!" Sir Harry darted his iron into the soft blubber clear to the hitches on the socket. The boat sped on out of danger of the twenty-foot wide flukes which immediately flashed thirty feet in the air and, coming down on the water with a sound like a volley of musketry, began churning the sea into suds.

The boat was hove to and the sail rolled around the mast which was unstepped and fleeted aft, the heel securely lodged under the after thwart and two-thirds of the mast sticking over the stern.

"Pull me up to him, my lads!" roared Sir Harry, gleefully, stripping the sheathe from a lance. "Lay me alongside and I'll operate on him with this overgrown surgical instrument."

The men hauled in the line smartly and brought the bow of the boat up to the whale well forward of his hump.

"Ah! Now I have him!" declared Sir Harry, and made a vigorous lunge with the lance.

In that mysterious manner a sperm whale exhibits at times, just as the lethal weapon flashed down, the bull sank like so much lead, the line whizzing around the loggerhead with such velocity as to set the stout piece of oak to smoking.

"Jove, I missed him!" deplored Sir Harry, recovering the lance with the warp attached to the handle. "There's more about this sport than I imagined, Captain."

Expert boat-headers waste no time in idle conjectures but are attending strictly to business every second when they are fast to a whale. It would have been well had Sir Harry done likewise, for, in the midst of his speculations, the bull made a sudden upward rush, his broad back lifting the bow of the boat high in the air.

Forthwith Sir Harry and the Sea Fox quitted the boat unceremoniously, the one being pitched frog-like over the bow and the other describing a parabola backward over the sternpost. The Sea Fox still retained his hold on the line which had a round turn on the loggerhead, and he was pulling himself hand over hand toward the boat when Sir Harry, striving desperately to disentangle himself from the line, bumped against him.

The slaver's iron grip fastened on the other's collar and supported him so that he was enabled to free his legs from the deadly line; for if the whale had started to run while Sir Harry was in that predicament he would have been cut in two.

"Thanks, Captain," panted the Englishman as they climbed back into the boat, which had settled back uninjured into the water.

"This is decidedly more interesting than hunting elephants, I'd say."

He had scarcely resumed his place in the bow when the bull slapped the sea mightily with his flukes, shoved his huge bulk partly out of water and, seemingly attracted by the glare of the setting sun, made for the western horizon at a pace that curled the sea a foot above the forward gunwales.

The Sea Fox threw another turn of the line over the logger-head and looked back to see how his other boat was faring. To his no little amusement, he saw that it had evidently been stoven at the first encounter and was now being hoisted to the slaver's davits. The *Crabtree's* boats had also fastened to whales and were now battling them close to the *Black Joke*, the crew of which was swarming in her rigging watching the contest. Cap'n Pepper experienced a feeling of uneasiness upon observing that another cruiser had put in an appearance further inshore. The bull, just then giving an additional spurt and straining the line, withdrew his attention from the newcomer and she, in fact everything but the business in hand, was forgotten in the exhilarating thrill of this "Nantucket sleighride."

The ships melted into the distance behind them and still the monstrous whale gave no signs of tiring. Finally, seeing that his enemy was still sticking to him like a burr, he decided on another course and, milling sharply 'round, headed back the way he had come.

For perhaps ten minutes he ran and then stopped dead, shoving his snoot perpendicularly out of water and taking a look 'round. In a moment he caught sight of the boat and, dropping his twenty-six foot lower jaw, bristling with huge ivory teeth, and belching an infuriated roar, he made a rush for the frail cedar craft.

By clever manipulation of his long steering-oar the Sea Fox avoided this onslaught, and, as the bull forged by, Sir Harry coolly buried the shining lance in him. By the merest chance, for neither he nor the Sea Fox had heard of the vulnerable spot, the lance plunged into the whale's "life", and his next spout was deeply crimsoned with blood.

The whale roared in agony as the razor-edged weapon again went home and in another moment thick blood was guttering from his spout-hole. Then the Sea Fox, suddenly remembering what the whaling captain had told him about a whale always going into a flurry just before dying, thought it prudent to withdraw the boat to a safe distance. He had barely done so when the bull made a half-breach and began dashing around in ever narrowing circles. Suddenly he stopped, gave a prolonged groan, and rolled over on his side, fin-out—dead.

BOOM! BOOM! The heavy reports of thirty-two-pounders startled the ears of the hunters and, lifting their exultant gaze from the dead whale and jerking their heads around, they beheld a truly astonishing sight—astonishing, at least, to Sir Harry.

Two cables' lengths away was the slaver-brigantine, tearing down before the wind and heading directly for them. Just out of range were the six cruisers in full chase behind, five of them under a cloud of canvas, the old *Firefly* belching smoke from her stack in a vain endeavor to keep in the race.

"Boollam Bill got to 'em at last," muttered the Sea Fox.

He waved his hand at Tom Dollar who was balancing himself on the rail and pointing down at the cutting-in stage that was now lowered at right-angles to the ship's side and about four feet above the water.

"Men, stan' by to catch that stage as she goes by!" Commanded the Sea Fox. "W'll leave the boat an' the whale to Sir Harry. I must say, sir, we was all mortal a-feared o' the *Black Joke*, 'count of hearin' so often that she could outsail us, but I see now she can't."

"But—but I don't understand!" stammered the bewildered naval captain. "Bless my soul, there's Commodore Gregory in the *Dale* firing at you again." A solid shot plumped into the water under the slaver's stern. "There must be some mistake."

"Gregory never makes no mistakes," grinned Cap'n Pepper. "Give him the Sea Fox's compliments when ye see him, please. An' I wanta thank ye for the pleasantest arternoon I ever see. Stan' by, boys. Here she is. Now! Catch her!"

SIR HARRY CLAVERING in his book "Black Ivory" finishes his narration of the slavers' escape with the following paragraphs of description:

> With her sky-scraping spars clothed with canvas from truck to deck, her great sails reflecting the red rays of the setting sun, she burst upon my startled gaze like a crimson cloud suddenly dropped from the skies. With her forefoot smoothly turning two furrows of liquid fire she swept down on our boat, a gigantic Negro steering at her wheel and fifty or more slaves squatting aft on top of her house to trim her by the stern.
>
> A lank, cadaverous individual stood on her rail by the main rigging, calmly munching tobacco and making signs for the slavers in the boat with me to catch hold of a wooden stage which projected nearly twenty feet out from her bends amidships. I had barely time to observe these details when the shadow of this towering, rushing fabric fell upon me and I crouched quickly to avoid the stage which stuck out as menacing as a scythe in the hub of a chariot.
>
> Of a sudden I felt the boat lighten and looking up, as the stern of the slaver flashed by me, I saw the Sea Fox and his four men clinging to the stage like so many flies.
>
> I was alone in the boat standing there watching the fleeing craft, fascinated, thrilling at this daring maneuver when the Sea Fox appeared on her poop by the taffrail. He waved his hand to me, not derisively, but, rather, as a hunter, going home at nightfall, turns and waves a farewell to the companion with whom he has borne the heat and burden of the day. In another moment this Napoleon of slavers had vanished from my sight, shut in by the purple dusk.

A TIP FROM JIM BOWIE

Far different from the Western haunts of Jim Bowie was this evil West African seaport, but, when his life and honor hung in the balance, the Sea Fox pinned his faith on the weapon and wisdom of the old plainsman

"**O**NE!" EXCLAIMED Cap'n Pepper, the Sea Fox. "Two!" announced Tom Dollar, the mate.

"Three!" chimed in Robin Hood, the huge black bosun.

Three puffs of blue smoke shot up, one after the other in rapid succession, from the west side of Grande Peak as the American slaver brigantine *Wild Pigeon* approached, just after sunrise, Princes Island (Lat. 1-38 N.; Lon. 7-25 W.) in the Gulf of Guinea.

The little lines of worry knitting the captain's brows vanished.

"That means the coast is clear; no cruisers prowling about," he observed, rapidly scanning the fretted row of peaks towering above dense forests of tropical trees in this volcanic flower garden. "Brace forrad a'gin, Robin Hood, an' if this wind holds we'll be in time to have breakfast with the Wider Ferraro an' Rosella."

He mused a moment.

"You'll mind, Tom Dollar, I told ye of the time the widder's daughter nussed me for six weeks after one o' them English Johnny Wars had blowed us outa water t'other side of that there p'int, when I was mate of the *Peggy Spur?* Well, ye see, I'd gone up in the main crosstrees to clear the signal halliards so's to get our flag down an' let them cussed Britishers know, we'd struck. Just then a red-hot shot plumps into our magazine an' the mast I'm on sails up into the air straight's a die, till I'm about on a level with the top o' that three thousand foot peak there, an' then we comes down so tarnal fast all the wind is drained plumb outa my body.

"Well, Tom Dollar, believe it or not, that mast swishes down—heel first, o' course, that end being the heaviest, an' buries itself for fifteen feet or more in the sandy beach. Sticks there as straight as a ramrod, an' me with my settin'-down place a-wedged into the arms o' the cross-trees so's I couldn't be shook off nohow. I didn't know all that happened after that, but when I got my bearings a'gin I was a-layin' in a room in Widder Ferraro's house an' her daughter, little Rosella—she was 'bout ten then—a-swabbin' my jowls with cold water.

"Seems I was the sole survivor, an' I'd probably 'a' passed 'the last frontier,' as the sayin' is, if the Widder an' Rosella hadn't nussed me so carefully; I was all shook up inside. Nat'rally I'm terrible fond of them two females, especially Rosella. She must be full-grown by this time. We ain't been here for two years or thereabouts. Keep her nor', nor'east," this to the helmsman. "An' Mr. Dollar, square yer fore yards; I'll tend to the mains'l, an' we'll run in between Piconegro P'int an' Carocha Island."

The Sea Fox slacked off the main sheet so that the boom would just clear the back-stays, and the beautiful clipper slaver, as if in answer to a rein, increased her speed and swept smoothly through the dark green water. The skipper went forward and, straddling his short, powerful legs on the fo'cas'le-head, conned her through the passage.

Past shaded heights down which dashed foaming cataracts the slavers sped, their nostrils titillating to the heavy scents from a thousand ripening fruits and flowers, until at eight o'clock they dropped anchor in twelve fathoms of water in East Bay.

Hardly had the ship put a strain on her cable when, leaving the efficient Robin Hood in charge, Cap'n Pepper and Tom Dollar went ashore in the dingy.

"Everythin' looks thrivin'," commented Cap'n Pepper as they stepped on the beach and he gazed up at the long, low, house of whitewashed brick partially hidden in a grove of orange trees and setting back some distance from the beach. "The Widder must be pretty well fixed. She owns two thirds o' this island an' she's got slaves enough to cultivate it. Yes, I reckon she's pretty comfortable. Well, I guess it ain't too early for us to pay our respects to her. Come on, Tom Dollar."

Half-way to the house the Sea Fox stopped suddenly beside a long Spanish thirty-two pounder half buried in the sand, a relic of the days when the island was a pirate resort.

"Funny we don't see nothin' o' Rosella, ain't it?" he remarked. "Right about here is where she allus used to come a-runnin' down to meet us, remember, Tom Dollar?"

The long, lanky mate tossed his quid carelessly into the rusted muzzle of the gun.

"Hell's flames, Cap'n; ye forgit she's older now," he replied. "She's prob'ly jest turned over for another nap. Them Portygee gals git mighty lazy when they get growed."

Cap'n Pepper shook his head, his broad, freckled face betraying not a little apprehension.

"Rosella ain't that kind. If she could she'd 'a' been here. Sunthin' must 'a' happened."

Something had, indeed. Five minutes later they found the Widow Ferraro, her eyes red from protracted weeping and her bosom still heaving from suppressed sobs.

Rosella had gone; vanished from the island two nights prior to the arrival of the Sea Fox.

IN HALTING, stifled phrases, with the tears coursing anew down her fat, doughy cheeks, the poor Portuguese mother told her American friends all she knew, concerning the sudden disappearance of her eighteen year old daughter. Stripped of all hysterical verbiage it amounted to this: a Spanish slaver brig, the *Emprendadora,* from Havana, bound to the African coast, and commanded by the notorious Captain Narcisco Guerra, had dropped anchor in East Bay on the preceding Wednesday. The widow had extended to him the hospitality of her house as she did all ship officers calling there. And she had supplied his ship with fruit and vegetables, for which he had paid liberally.

Captain Guerra had sailed sometime Thursday night, and the following morning Rosella was missing. The island had been combed high and low, but no trace of the girl had been found and her mother was therefore fully convinced that Guerra had abducted her.

During the silence which followed this recital the Sea Fox produced a quill toothpick from a pocket and chewed it thoughtfully.

"Did Rosella take anything with her?" he asked finally.

"Nothing but what she stood in. That's what makes me believe that Captain Guerra took her away forcibly," replied the widow.

"Did Guerra say what factory he was a-goin' to?" asked the Sea Fox, after pondering over this for a while.

"No."

"Your men didn't see nothin' around the decks that would give any idee where she was bound, did they? No cases marked with the consignee's name or such like, Mrs. Ferraro?"

"No." She thought a moment or two and then added despondently, "I have questioned all of them; there was nothing like that. The only distinctive thing about the brig I remember was Rosella's telling me that she was very much amused at a large gray parrot in the cabin that was continually calling, 'cha-cha,' 'cha-cha,' or some such senseless thing."

"Cha-cha!" repeated the Sea Fox, clamping his heavy jaws on

the toothpick. "That word mebbe ain't so silly as it sounds." He cast a meaning glance at his mate, who nodded his head as if in answer to a question.

Cap'n Pepper glanced at his watch.

"It is now 8:53. By ten o'clock I wanta be gittin' my anchor," he told Mrs. Ferraro. "An' I wish you would kindly hustle up yer men an' keep putting fresh provisions aboard up to that time. An' ye might have some o' your help put some fodder on that table at the end o' the veranda where me an' my mate ate when we was here last. We'd certainly 'preciate it."

The widow's dark eyes flashed gratefully. This abrupt departure could mean but one thing—the Sea Fox was going to look for her daughter. This and the latent power suggested by every movement of this stocky, five-foot-five slaver comforted and put new heart into her. As quickly as she could raise her stout figure from her chair she hastened to do his bidding.

The two slavers, left alone, sat in silence, the Sea Fox grinding away at the toothpick, his shaggy brows knitted in deep thought.

Two slave girls came and began laying the table with snow-white linen and old-fashioned silverware. This done they motioned for the slavers to take their seats and almost immediately set before them curried eggs and a steaming platter of savory chicken ragout. A large pot of coffee mingled its fragrant aroma with the delicious scents from the flowers in the garden.

Finally, with a grateful sigh, the Sea Fox tilted back in his chair and produced another quill toothpick.

"Tom Dollar, what are ye a-thinkin' on?" he asked abruptly.

"The same thing you be, Cap'n," grinned the mate.

"An' what is that, Tom Dollar?"

"Hell's flames! Anyone can see ye're all he't up about that there parrot on the *Emprendadora* bawlin' 'cha-cha' all the time. Ain't it a fact?"

"You've hit it, Tom Dollar. An' what d'yer make of it?"

"Why, it's all as plain's a tar-pot in a bar'l o' flour to me, Cap'n. Guerra got that parrot from Cha-cha of Ayudah."

"Exactly, Tom Dollar," agreed the Sea Fox, with an admiring glance at his mate.

There was a long pause, during which each was engaged in searching the tablets of his memory in an effort to recall all that he had heard about this remarkable trader, Señor Da Souza, better known on the coast as Cha-cha.

But all the slavers knew about him was that he was a native mulatto from Brazil; that he had deserted from the Brazilian army and shipped on a slaver for Dahome. Here after some terrible adventures, he had finally won the favor of the rich King of Dahome and had now become the second most opulent factor on the coast. His was a one-man town and he was that man. Striving to emulate the gaudy court of his protector, the king, he had everything that could add to the pleasures of human existence brought from London, Paris, and Havana and offered for sale in Ayudah. In short, he had surrounded himself with all that could corrupt virtue, gratify passion, tempt avarice, betray weakness, satisfy sensuality, and complete a picture of incarnate slavery in Dahome.

As all this floated through the mind of the Sea Fox he groaned audibly.

"Tom Dollar," he announced solemnly, "if Rosella had s'arched all through hell she couldn't 'a' found a worse place than she's boun' for now. Nor two greater mates of the devil than this Cha-cha an' that Spaniard, Guerra. I dunno so much about the Spaniard, he's only been running slaves about three years an' has never crossed my hawse; but from what I've heard o' him he's a bad egg. He's a bully an' a braggart, but he ain't a coward by no means. They say he don't know what fear is an' I guess that's right for he's a reg'lar shark at fightin' duels. He's already killed six men that way, Tom Dollar."

"I know. I heerd 'bout it," returned the mate.

"Now," continued the Sea Fox, "I dunno which is the prime mover in this here case, Cha-cha or Guerra. But I b'lieve if Rosella's been stole it's Cha-cha's doing, for I don't think Guerra would go that far without heavy backin'." He got on his feet. "We'd better be gettin' under way, right now, Tom Dollar, an' make Ayudah as quick's God an' the wind 'll let us."

While taking leave of the Widow Ferraro the Sea Fox said, "I can't tell ye my plans, Mrs. Ferraro, for I dunno myself jest yet how I'm a-goin' to work. But; I aim to kill two birds with one stun', get Rosella an' my cargo at the same time, see? So don't worry no more'n ye can help. If it's a possible thing you'll have yer gal back safe an' sound soon. Come on, Tom Dollar."

To avoid the mother's trembling thanks he pulled the mate hastily down the veranda steps with him, and in a little while they were mounting the side of their ship.

The *Wild Pigeon* made the run of four hundred and thirty miles in fifty-one hours, having light winds part of the way. At four o'clock on a Tuesday afternoon in June she brought up to her anchor in the open roadstead of Ayudah. A cable's length away were the raking masts and black, swan-like hull of the Spanish slaver *Emprendadora.*

THE SEA FOX smiled as he read her name through his glasses.

"Mr. Parrot," he declaimed aloud, "you was a bird o' good omen."

"Hell's flames, I hope so," agreed Tom Dollar heartily. Then his naturally long face lengthened. "But I jest can't figger out how ye're a-goin' to get to win'ard of Guerra an' fill up with slaves at the same time. Not as tight as we be right now."

It was a fact. They were extremely hard pressed. Business reverses suffered by the vessel's New York owner, Calvin Gale, had compelled the ship to sail with sufficient specie and trade goods to buy only one fifth of the cargo she could carry. It had been the Sea Fox's intention to consign his ship to his friend, Duke Ephraim of Old Calabar, who would have extended him credit on his note. Now the Rosella episode had forced him to discard this plan.

"It's a mess, I'll admit," conceded Cap'n Pepper. "I never had no dealin's with this here Cha-cha, an' he ain't the kind o' man I'd ask any favors of if I had. But leave it to me, Tom Dollar, I ain't been pacin' the deck half the night since we left Princes Island for nothin'."

Cha-cha had built a palatial residence near the site of an old abandoned Portuguese fort. A large gambling casino stood a hundred yards or so further west. This near-palace and gambling hell, as well as the other houses of the little town, were painted an immaculate white and were roofed with tiles of a dull yellow. It was evident, at a glance, that no expense had been spared to make this African Monte Carlo a haven of luxurious rest for the tired slaver coming in with his hold full of trade goods and specie.

Through his glasses the Sea Fox could see guests seated at tables on the verandas of Cha-cha's house sipping their wine; but the surf was roaring inshore as high as a three-story house, thundering and lathering on the broad beach so that landing was impossible, for some hours at least.

Cap'n Pepper's chief anxiety was for Rosella. As soon as possible he sent his steward, Vicente, a diplomatic New Orleans Spaniard, aboard the *Emprendadora* to learn all he could about the girl. Nothing is more natural than for one steward to visit another, whereas had the Sea Fox gone himself it would have undoubtedly excited comment that would have reached Guerra's ears. This the American slaver wished to avoid for the present.

Vicente returned about dusk and reported that Guerra had taken Rosella ashore immediately upon the arrival of the vessel on Monday morning and that the *Emprendadora's* steward was firmly convinced that Miss Ferraro was desperately in love with the handsome Spanish captain.

Whatever the Sea Fox thought about this he kept to himself, but showed a decided interest when Vicente further informed him that Guerra had come to the coast well provided with specie and that in consequence Cha-cha had promised him a quick dispatch.

"Which means I gotta get busy," decided Cap'n Pepper.

The surf subsiding during the night, the next morning, at eight o'clock, Cha-cha dispatched a canoe for the *Wild Pigeon's* captain. The latter was well known by reputation to this African nabob, though the two had never met. As the American was reputed to have made several successful voyages, Cha-cha surmised that he had plenty of money and had undoubtedly come to Ayudah with a fat invoice.

Accordingly the reception of the Sea Fox by this hollow-cheeked, sodden-eyed mulatto was effusive in the extreme. He insisted that the American should make the big house his headquarters during his stay in port and promised, with a sly wink, that the captain should not suffer for the want of entertainment.

Cap'n Pepper, knowing his man, politely declined the other's flattering offers. His ship was his home, he said, and after pretending to be greatly impressed by the trader's striking personality he excused himself for a while and went off for a stroll.

The Sea Fox spoke Spanish and a half-dozen coast dialects with almost the fluency of the native, and, by a tip bestowed judiciously here and there, he soon found himself in front of a house in a street back of the Casino, partially surrounded by a grove of high palm-pines. Two rows of paw-paw trees bordered the fifty-foot path which led up to the veranda.

Swaggering down this path to the street was a tall, well set-up Spaniard of about thirty-five, who, despite his foppish attire, bore the marks of a sailor.

His long black eyes, hard and bright as enamel, narrowed a little as they flashed on the American, and his carefully curled mustache lifted in a half sneer as he swung by.

"A reg'lar rearin', tearin' swashbuckler ye think ye be, don't ye?" was Cap'n Pepper's mental reservation as he watched the broad shoulders and trim waist of the Spaniard disappear around the corner. "That's Guerra, all right, from the description I've had give me. Well, ye child-snatcher ye, I've an' idee we'll be better 'quainted afore long."

He began walking up the path toward the house when he suddenly caught sight of a large girl, plump almost to stoutness, staring at him with wide eyes from her post on the edge of the veranda. It was Rosella.

S H E W A S dressed in a gown of glaring yellow silk and wore a large bow of the same material and color in her black hair, which was coarse and thick as a mane. Beautiful she was not, her heavy countenance being redeemed only by a pair of magnificent black eyes and a clear olive complexion.

Her voice caught in an exclamation of delight not unmixed with a shade of consternation as the Sea Fox came up to her.

"Capitan Pepper!" she cried. *"Es posible?"* With the impulsiveness of her Latin nature she flung her arms around his thick neck and kissed him warmly on either cheek.

The captain laughed as she finally disengaged herself and, leaning back against a hammock, surveyed him with an air of smiling bewilderment.

"Must be possible, Rosella, seein' that here I be," he answered, slumping easily into a chair. "Mighty han'some gal ye got to be since I seen ye last, I must say. But ain't ye a long ways from home, Rosella?"

The girl bent her head, her fingers playing nervously with the string of amber beads about her neck.

"Of course I dunno's it's any o' my bus'ness but nat'rally I'm considerable interested in the gal that nussed me through that sickness o' mine. An' another thing, Rosella," he fixed her with his piercing eyes, "yer mother is plumb worried to death about ye."

At the mention of her mother the girl's eyes filled and within the next ten minutes he had the story.

She had eloped with Guerra, who, according to her, was the personification of beauty, generosity, and kindness. His attitude toward her throughout had been that rare combination of lover and brother; they were to be married as soon as he got his cargo of slaves.

"How soon will that be?" asked the Sea Fox, pricking up his ears.

"Cha-cha promises them in four days," she counted on her fingers, "that will be about Monday. And then—"

She clasped her hands raptly.

The Sea Fox sighed.

At this juncture an old Soosoo woman, of an ashy dark color and wrinkled like a nutmeg, appeared in the doorway and gave him an evil stare before she scuttled back into the house.

"Who was that ant'deluvian critter?" asked the Sea Fox.

"That is Kyer, my *duenna*, and," she added proudly, "Narcisco has already given me two slave girls."

Cap'n Pepper grunted and switched the conversation to reminiscences of her island home. After another ten minutes he rose and held out his hand.

"Ye seem to be all right so far, Rosella; but in case any 'mergency rises don't forget that yer mother is spendin' some little time every day on her knees about ye," he said. "Good day."

Cap'n Pepper walked thoughtfully up the street, pondering on his next move. He had not gone very far when, as luck would have it, he ran into an old acquaintance, Mafucca John, a slave broker whom he had known in bygone days around Bonny. From him the Sea Fox learned that Guerra had already, during the past two years, furnished Cha-cha's harem and Casino with several girls whom he had brought to Ayudah in precisely the same manner as he had Rosella.

Cap'n' Pepper lunched with the broker and then, taking his leave, made his way down to the slave barracoons in the northwest part of the town. Here again he found it necessary to dip into his pocket, whereupon the captain of the barracooniers, or slavemaster, melted into a state of graciousness and showed his visitor about.

In the barracoon alloted to the *Emprendadora* were already

two hundred and fifty slaves, fine husky creatures, with the exception of two which the expert eye of the Sea Fox noted had been doctored with a mixture of gunpowder and lemon-juice to make them look plump and shiny. Only the yellow eyeballs and swollen tongue showed the cheat.

"What would ye say now if ye wanted to call a man some partic'ly bad names?" inquired the Sea Fox as he was about to go.

The slave-master grinned. "A man gets pretty good at that in this business, Captain. I would begin by calling him a coward, a poltroon, a liar, a slanderer of the unfortunate, a grave-robber, a—"

"Good'nough!" chuckled Cap'n Pepper. "That's the real p'izen an' no mistake. Now, does Cap'n Guerra ever come down here?"

"Yes. I expect him in an hour or so. He comes every afternoon. He's a gay dog is Captain Guerra, but he tends to business."

"That's fine. Now listen careful. When he comes ye jest call him all them names ye jest mentioned an' as much more's ye can think on, an' tell him that's what Cap'n Pepper said he is."

The slave-master's eyeballs protruded in astonishment. He looked at the American aghast.

"Why, Captain," he cried, "I won't do that. It would be your sentence to death. Captain Guerra would immediately call you out and kill you. He's a regular fire-eater of the *code duello*. I myself saw him kill two opponents on the beach right abreast of your own vessel, Captain, and they say he has killed at least seven more in Havana."

"I know all about that," interposed the Sea Fox, "an' I don't s'pose I'm any match for Guerra. But jest the same I gotta have my little joke. An' I'm mighty glad Guerra is so all-fired touchy, for it ain't no fun stirrin' up a man with no spirit. Now ye jest do as I ask ye an' ye won't lose by it."

The sudden pressure of a gold piece on the palm of his hand swept away the slavemaster's scruples and he promptly agreed to do as the slaver desired.

After learning of two other resorts which Guerra frequented the Sea Fox took his departure.

"You may think it is going to be a good joke, my fine Captain," observed the slave-master, looking at the slaver's retreating figure, "but God help you when Guerra hunts you out, as he will surely do. Well, it is none of my affair. You've paid me to do it and I will."

HE DID, as did the two proprietors of the other resorts whom the Sea Fox had paid to do the same thing. Cap'n Pepper could not have chosen better emissaries for his purpose. All of the three cordially hated the arrogant, swaggering bully, and this chance to tell him to his face what they thought of him without danger to their own skins was too good to be lost.

Accordingly the three deputies spent all of the time until Guerra put in an appearance in recalling the most insulting vilifications which their memories had retained after years of intercourse with a class who have reduced calumny to a fine art. Trust a Spaniard or a Portuguese for applying the acid with a serene deftness.

"Really, Captain Guerra, such an extraordinary request. The Americano must be insane. At first I refused. I warned him of your prowess, dear Captain Guerra; but he insisted that I tell you in his very words—" And then began the broadside.

When at four o'clock he burst out, with flaming eyes, from the last resort, there was not a madder man from the Senegal to the Congo than Captain Narcisco Guerra. Rosella had informed him of the captain's visit that morning and Guerra, in consequence, at once jumped to the conclusion that this covert attack on the part of the American was the result of jealousy; without a doubt Cap'n Pepper wanted Rosella for himself.

For over an hour Guerra strode agitatedly up one street and down another, looking into all the places where a sea-faring man would be likely to go; but he saw no sign of the Sea Fox. Meanwhile the man he was raving to meet was reclining at his ease under a big cotton tree, secure from prying eyes but where he could see plainly the gate of Guerra's barracoon. To judge by the placid expression of his countenance one could hardly believe that he had, of his own free will, deliberately started a game, the stakes of which were the biggest a man can ever play for—his own life, and a friend's honor.

A little before sundown the Sea Fox got slowly to his feet.

"Lemme see, now," he mused, fixing his eyes on a tiny gray monkey that had been seated on the lower limb of an adjacent tree for the last hour.

"Accordin' to what the slave-master told me an' what I've seen myself, there's been sixty slaves gone into Guerra's barracoon this day. If they keeps coming in at this rate he'll get his complement of five hundred and fifty about Sat'day sometime, instead of Monday as Rosella thought. Now five hundred and fifty slaves will fill up the *Wild Pigeon* nicely, very nicely indeed. So far, so good. *Adios* Mrs. Monk; I'm a-goin' to see what sorta grub this Cha-cha pervides—that is, if I don't run foul o' Guerra a-thirs-tin' for my gore."

The dying sun swept his path with a purple splendor as he made his way into the town. He chuckled to himself as he noticed the looks of awed surprise bestowed on him by pedes-trians he met, for the news had spread like wild-fire that the Yankee slaver captain had had the suicidal rashness to wantonly insult the terrible Guerra.

The startled looks of these people, with the interest he excited among the patrons of the eating place, convinced him that his last three tips had borne abundant fruit. This was confirmed when Captain Walters, the bluff, hearty skipper of a Liverpool bark lying in the harbor, took a seat at the same table.

"I don't think you'll take it amiss, Captain, if I tell you that Guerra is hunting high and low for you," he said, after intro-ducing himself. "That Spaniard is bad enough at any time, but he's half-drunk now and ready for anything. I merely wanted to let you know how the thing stands and put you on your guard."

The Sea Fox thanked him.

"Jest a little joke o' mine, Cap'n," he explained; "that Spanish dandy sorta riled me this mornin; when I see him a-blusterin' about as if he owned all creation, so I guessed I'd have a little fun with him. That is all."

The English skipper looked at him quizzically for a long moment, mentally concluding that this Yankee, whose crag-like features were as impressive as so much granite, was either as cunning as his nickname implied or else he was a consummate idiot. The Englishman was more inclined to the former supposition until, a little later in the evening, something happened that left him completely in the air, hardly knowing what to think.

NIGHT FELL. The soft sky was star-gemmed and the land breeze, which had set in at sundown, soothingly fanned the cheeks of the two skippers as they left the place and picked their way across the square to the Casino, now ablaze with lights.

This gambling establishment was one big room a hundred and twenty feet long, and fifty wide. It was lighted by three immense chandeliers and by oil lamps in gilded brackets placed along the walls. All the paraphernalia for gaming was here and also two billiard tables. And in the back part of the room was a mahogany bar presided over by two silk-shirted bartenders, who spoke half a dozen languages.

As the Sea Fox and his companion entered, there arose a hum of voices like the sound of bees swarming above their hive, but the play went on as usual. Cha-cha, accompanied by his body-guard of two of the dreadful Amazons of Kumasi, greeted them cordially. He knew, of course, what was in the minds of all present, but so far it was no business of his.

The two mariners sat down on a lounge about midway on the west side of the room and began watching the animated scene, the Britisher smoking a cigar and the Sea Fox chewing nonchalantly on the inevitable quill toothpick. Beautiful half-caste women, clad in Paris gowns, strolled about the vast room, attentive to their business of luring lookers-on to try their luck at the tables; it was significant that not one of them approached the Sea Fox. Indeed it seemed that since his entrance there had been a deadening of the atmosphere; the sort of stifling calm that presages the hurricane.

For half an hour nothing happened. Then, of a sudden, there came the sound of a high neighing laugh, and the tall form of Guerra appeared between the heavy, green plush portiers which hung across the wide arched doorway. The Spanish captain had evidently dressed for the occasion. He sported a new white beaver hat, and he wore a scarlet jacket ornamented down the front with a double row of solid gold buttons and stopping just short of a broad red and blue silk sash. This contained a pair of silver mounted pistols and also concealed the belt that upheld the silver-hilted cutlass hanging down his left leg. The laces of his slashed trousers bottoms were fastened to tiny gold buttons, the last one of which was reflected in patent leather boots of the latest design.

He stood there in the doorway, glancing about the room until all were enabled to have a good look at his magnificent presence, and then advanced with rapid strides toward the Sea Fox. Instantly all play was suspended, the room became hushed, and Cap'n Pepper at once became the center of attraction.

"Here comes Guerra! Look out now. He means mischief," whispered the Britisher to the Sea Fox, who, with his hands resting on his thick, muscular legs, was staring straight before him but taking in everything out of the corner of his eye.

" 'Sall right. Cap'n," he rejoined. "I gotta face the music, I s'pose. I can't get away from him now nohow."

The next instant Guerra stood before them, the light from the chandeliers blazing in a myriad of rays from the polished buttons. There was a loud stir as the players at the tables rose from their seats and craned their necks.

Shifting the toothpick from one side of his mouth to the other, the Sea Fox looked up into the glaring eyes of the Spaniard whose thin features were twitching with rage, his upper lip drawn up so that the ends of his mustache were well above the wings of his nostrils. He hissed like a snake as he prepared to give vent to his fury.

"Get to one side, will ye?" requested the Sea Fox, in Spanish, his deep voice booming through the room. "Ye're a-standin' in my way. I can't see."

A murmur of admiration went up from the assemblage. The American was running true to form.

Tongue-tied with passion and with flecks of foam appearing on his lower lip, Guerra stooped and spat squarely into the eyes of the Sea Fox.

"Can you see better now?" he shrilled.

THEN HIS long arm shot out and, clutching the other's collar, he jerked him to his feet. After shaking the Sea Fox as a terrier does a rat, Guerra administered the crowning insult, two kicks delivered with all his force.

Wrenching himself loose, Cap'n Pepper backed toward the door as Cha-cha came running up and the two Amazons crossed their spears before the frenzied Guerra.

"Gentlemen, gentlemen," cautioned Cha-cha, "you know the rules; no quarreling in the rooms."

At the door the Sea Fox stopped and, after wiping his face calmly with a handkerchief, addressed the disappointed audience, who had expected, at the least, a challenge given and accepted.

"I want ye to understan', folks, that I don't retract a word I said about this cuss," Cap'n Pepper said. "He's all I said he is an' more. An' I tell ye right now that if I wasn't troubled with rheumatiz I might fight him."

"My God!" ejaculated the British skipper, and threw the butt of his cigar vehemently into a spittoon.

Cap'n Pepper's little speech was greeted with hoots, groans and bursts of derisive laughter. Guerra endeavored anew to get by the Amazons and pursue the Sea Fox, who, just then, disappeared through the door.

"Don't be foolish, Captain Guerra," Cha-cha murmured in his ear. "If you kill him now you get nothing but his life. Let the matter rest in my hands and I think we can get him and that splendid vessel of his besides."

Guerra's temporary madness had not effected his natural acquisitiveness in the least, and he gradually became quite calm. After all, was he not the hero of the hour; had he not exposed the famous Sea Fox and proved him to be nothing but a monstrous bluffer? So he adjourned to the bar with Cha-cha and some captains whose vessels were anchored along the bight waiting for trade.

"Them bloody Yankees is nothing but a lot o' bloomin' bags of wind," declared one of them. "How'd he get that name o' Sea Fox, I'd like to know?"

"Why, Captain, can't you see?" answered another. "The name is most appropriate. A fox never fights, you know; it just steals something and runs away with it."

A roar of laughter followed this sally and glasses clinked.

"By gar!" chimed in a French skipper, wiping his immensely long mustaches. "You say de Sea Fox no fight, eh? I say de man must be seek tonight. You forget, gentlemeen, how t'ree year ago he make the *Amitista* strike her colors, I theenk."

At this the group were suddenly struck dumb, staring in some perplexity at one another, for there was no gainsaying the fact that the Sea Fox had decisively beaten off the Spanish man-of-war in question despite her heavier armament and greater number of men.

Cha-cha broke the silence.

"There are different phases of bravery, gentlemen," he commented in his easy, graceful way. "The Sea Fox is brave, undoubtedly, when he is backed up by that fighting crew of his and those two officers that are as good as ten ordinary men. *Si*, but in the duel where there is no cheering, no stimulating smell of gunpowder—ah, gentlemen, he shrinks from that. You all saw tonight. The idea of going out on that beach alone to fight a man like Captain Guerra was too much for him. It is the *code duello* that shows a man in his true colors, for it is a fact that never does a pistol look grimmer or steel so naked as when one man is facing another on the field of honor."

Here Guerra joined in, swearing that he would never rest satisfied until he had wiped out the insult in Cap'n Pepper's blood, and that he would take such measures as would force the bluffer to fight him.

At this juncture a self-effacing little man with the dark complexion of a Spaniard quietly emptied his glass and glided unnoticed from the room. It was Vicente, the steward of the *Wild Pigeon.*

Meanwhile Cap'n Pepper had procured a canoe and been taken off to the ship.

"Hullo, is that you, Cap'n?" asked Tom Dollar, advancing through the darkness of the poop to meet him. "Any good news, Cap'n?"

"The best, Tom Dollar. It mebbe is a little soon to say it yet, but, if I'm any judge, I calculate on being bound out afore this time next week with Rosella aboard an' a full cargo o' slaves. How does that strike ye?"

"Hell's flames! It hits me to a T, Cap'n. But I'm damned if I see how ye're a-goin' to do it."

"Well, I see, Tom Dollar; so jest leave it to me."

Half an hour later Vicente came aboard and reported to his master the discussion which had ensued upon Cap'n Pepper's abject retirement. The Sea Fox chuckled and then told Vicente that until further orders he was relieved from all his duties as steward and that he was to remain ashore during the daytime, checking up on the slaves entering Guerra's barracoon and trying to ascertain the identity and addresses of the girls that Guerra had consigned to the hectic life of Ayudah.

Early the next morning the Sea Fox sent the boat ashore to fill two gunny-sacks with the fine beach sand. Until the boat returned he busied himself making a bag of light canvas, about six feet long and, when filled, about the diameter of the body of an average man. When the sand was brought he mixed some of it with farina—cereal slave-food—carefully weighing it on the scales as he added more farina, until, when the bag was filled and sewn up, it was the exact weight he desired, one hundred and eighty pounds.

"I b'lieve the Old Man has gone clean crazy!" ejaculated Tom Dollar as, some twenty minutes later, he happened to look down through the skylight into the cabin and descried a most remarkable scene. Flat on his back in the middle of the carpet lay Cap'n Pepper, and, as the mate stared, he saw Robin Hood pick up the heavy bag and toss it on the prostrate form of the skipper. Had it landed on him, it would undoubtedly have done some injury. While it was still in the air, however, the captain's powerful legs shot up and intercepted it with the soles of his boots.

Cap'n Pepper continued this curious practice at regular intervals during that and the next day, until at last he could juggle the bag with the ease and dexterity of a circus clown doing the same thing with a ball.

At three o'clock that afternoon Cha-cha came aboard, bearing a challenge from Guerra to meet him on the beach in mortal combat; as an inducement for the American to fight him the Spaniard offered to wager the valuation of the *Wild Pigeon* in gold coin against the vessel itself, winner take all.

"Humph!" the Sea Fox burst out. "I think I see yer hand in this, Cha-cha. Wanta have my life an' vessel too, do ye? Ye know mighty well what sorta chance I stan' ag'in Guerra. He's a dead shot an' I can't hit a barn door; an' they say he eats with a sword. No sir, Cha-cha, I value my life more'n that. Ye go back an' tell Guerra he'll have to increase his offer some considerable afore he'll get a chance to show his dexterity on me."

Cha-cha went back and reported this to Guerra.

"We shall never get him to fight you," mourned the mulatto, "not if I should offer him the whole town. He is a coward to his very marrow. But we will see what we can do."

On the following afternoon, Friday, Guerra sent off a messenger with a letter to the Sea Fox. It implored him, if he had a spark of manhood left, to fight and to arrange the meeting as expeditiously as possible for Guerra's complement of slaves was about complete and he would have to sail very soon. The Spaniard wound up his epistle by offering to stake all of the slaves in his barracoon against the *Wild Pigeon* on the result of the combat. This was a powerful incentive, indeed, but the Sea Fox apparently betrayed but little interest.

"Go back," he told the messenger, "an' tell Guerra I'll give him my answer afore eight o'clock tonight."

Just before sundown Vicente came aboard to report.

"Keep the canoe alongside," said the Sea Fox, "I'll be sendin' ye ashore ag'in soon with a note. What ye got to tell me?"

Vicente informed him that there were now five hundred and thirty slaves in Guerra's barracoon and that he had also learned the whereabouts of four girls who owed their present condition to the Spaniard.

After hearing this Cap'n Pepper scribbled a note to Cha-cha and sent the steward to deliver it. Cha-cha read the note aloud on the floor of the Casino and it created quite a sensation. It ran:

Señor De Souza:
  You and Guerra meet me and my second tomorrow morning at seven o'clock, in your private room, and we will talk turkey.
                    Cap't. B. Pepper.

THE NOTE dispatched, Cap'n Pepper got into the dingy and pulled over to the Liverpool bark. Captain Walters met him at the gang-way with a cold stare.

"What can I do for you, sir?" he asked icily. "I have some accounts to go over, so please state your business in the shortest time and the quickest manner possible."

The Sea Fox grinned. "I jest come over, Cap'n, to tell ye that the time is come to give that Spaniard what he's a-hollerin' for, an' I want ye to be my second."

"By George, I'm your man!" cried the Britisher, with glistening eyes and grasping his visitor by the hand. "My time and everything I've got is yours. Come below, my dear fellow."

Half an hour was spent in the cabin discussing the various points of the coming affray and then the Sea Fox went back to his ship.

An hour before dawn, the next morning, the crew of the *Wild Pigeon* were roused and the guns double-shotted. The men were then dismissed and aft on the poop Cap'n Pepper informed his officers of the coming duel.

"If I get killed," he continued, "you'll be cap'n, Tom Dollar, an' whatever arrangements I might 'a' made with them sharks ashore is null an' void. The fight'll take place on the beach where ye can easily see ever'thin' with the glasses. If ye see my second wavin' a red han'kercher you'll know that I'm done for an' ye are at once to slip yer cable an' run to sea. If ye see me wave a white one ye haul taut on that spring ye got to the cable so's yer broadside will cover the town an' then await further orders. Oh, I forgot—if ye should have to go to sea without me, run down to Old Calabar an' do the best ye can there for Calvin Gale. That's all."

Daylight came. A little before seven the Sea Fox and the British captain appeared at Cha-cha's house. The Britisher was carrying under his arm what looked to be a small case of surgical instruments.

"You won't have to do any doctoring, Captain," remarked Guerra, casting a scowl at the Sea Fox. "I always do a good job."

"Now, gentlemen!" protested Cha-cha. "We are here to arrange matters quietly. There will be plenty of time for the other afterward. Come this way please."

He led the way to his office. On the table in the middle of the room were two shining cutlasses, already sharpened, and a pair of large-bore duelling pistols.

"Now," began Cha-cha, when they were seated. "Our first business, I believe, Captain Walters is to write out an agreement binding the stakes. That there may be no mistake, I cite them. Captain Guerra bets his five hundred and thirty, slaves against Captain Pepper's vessel, the *Wild Pigeon,* that he wins the combat which is to go to the end. Is that right, Captain Walters?"

The latter nodded and Cha-cha, calling for his clerk, had two copies of the agreement made out, keeping one himself and handing the other to Cap'n Pepper's second. Dismissing the clerk, Cha-cha broached the subject of weapons.

"Captain Pepper, as the challenged party, has the choice of weapons. There are some splendid ones there on the table, and, each pair being just alike, it—"

"Show 'em what I'm a-goin to fight with, Cap'n," the Sea Fox cut in, turning to his second.

The Britisher rose and, unrolling the leather case on the table, displayed two heavy bowie-knives with glittering twelve-inch blades—beauties that assuredly would have delighted the eye of Jim Bowie himself.

Cha-cha stared aghast at the lethal instruments a moment, then leaned toward Guerra.

"I've an idea we have been fooled in some manner I cannot fathom," he whispered.

Guerra tossed his head impatiently and sprang to his feet, his arched nostrils dilating with the blood-lust as his eyes rested on the shining steel. He had fought with knives before and liked the feel of one in his hand. Moreover, he had all the advantage, for he was seven inches taller than his opponent and had at least three inches more of reach.

"You couldn't have suited me better!" he snarled. "I came here to fight; knives or cannon, it is all the same to me. Come down to the beach and get it over quickly." He threw a triumphant look at the Sea Fox. "I'm to be married to Rosella at noon and have little time to spare. Come on."

Captain Walters rolled up the knives again and the party made their way to the beach. Here the Britisher, as second to the challenged one, took charge. He had Cha-cha send for a coil of rope and a space fifty feet square was roped off to keep back the crowd that was surging down to the beach; the news had gone forth that the great fight was about to take place. Captain Walters insisted that no one be allowed between the combatants and the sea, which was agreed to without question.

THERE WAS not a cloud in the sky; the morning mist had also vanished, drunk up by the burning sun.

The two prepared for battle. The Sea Fox stripped to his undershirt and trousers which were held up by a belt. To prevent his trousers from slipping down in case the belt should be severed he had stitched the waistband to the undershirt with stout sail-twine. He wore the same glove-fitting calf-skin boots with the heavy soles and heels that he had worn while practising with the sand bag.

Captain Guerra doffed his gay jacket and rolled the sleeves of his silk shirt above the elbows of his sinewy arms. The Britisher felt over him for steel mesh and Cha-cha made a similar examination of the Sea Fox.

The combatants were handed their knives and stationed five paces from each other. For the last time, with a movement of his eyes nearly as swift as the click of a camera, the Sea Fox took in the scene: the palm-shaded little town, the broad sweep of silvery beach, the flashing of innumerable eyes as their excited owners crowded the ropes, the shimmering sea, and his beloved vessel and the flag under which so many bloody battles had been fought, flying from her peak.

"Are you all ready, gentlemen?" asked Captain Walters.

"Jest a second!" enjoined the Sea Fox. "You, Guerra, I think it but fair ye should know why I took so much pains to rile ye. Marm Ferraro is a friend of mine, for one reason; an' the other is that I wanted them slaves o' yourn. I'm all ready, Cap'n."

"Go!" shouted the seconds, removing their hands from the principals' shoulders and hurriedly stepping back out of the way.

"This is going to be a bloody wicked fight," observed a cockney captain; "they're both hard as nails and can stand lots of cutting."

Then as Guerra leaped toward the Sea Fox a hush fell over the crowd, broken only by the sobbing of the surf.

With right arm easily extended and slowly moving the blade of his knife like the tail of a snake, Guerra circled about his adversary. Cap'n Pepper's sturdy body revolved slowly, in unison with the methodical movement of a capstan, his knife held, point out, half way down his right leg. Guerra, always the aggressor, suddenly changed his tactics to a series of jumps and feigned attacks, until, seeing an opening, he gave a tigerish spring, the knife in his hand sweeping like a scythe.

The Sea Fox leaped to one side, but not quite far enough to avoid the razor edged blade. It slashed the undershirt beneath his left arm and made a slight cut. Worse followed. Apparently losing his balance in his effort to avoid the knife, the Sea Fox stumbled and fell flat on his back. In his apparent attempt to break the fall his own knife hand sank in the sand, carrying the weapon with it to the hilt, so that only the blade poked ineffectually above the ruffled floor of the beach.

A groan, deep as the rumbling of a great organ, went up from the spectators. Many turned their heads away. It was all over. In that position a man is absolutely at the mercy of his adversary. All the latter has to do is to plant his foot on the knife-arm of the fallen one and shove home the steel. Quick to take advantage of the seeming helplessness of the Sea Fox, with one bound Guerra was beside him. Cap'n Pepper threw his left arm over his face as if to ward off the sight of the lethal steel.

The long body of the Spaniard bent over him, shutting out the sun. Up went the knife. At the pause, the split second of time ere it descended, the legs of the Sea Fox, round and hard as bollards, flashed inward and then shot up, landing those stout-soled boots with terrific force into the pit of the other's stomach.

Guerra gave a horrible grunt, while his face turned an ashen color and the knife flew from his hand.

Hardly crediting their own eyes, the spectators watched with bated breath while those trained legs tossed the Spaniard spread-eagled in the air and then let him fall on the Sea Fox's knife, held waiting for him on the sand.

Rolling the body off, the Sea Fox got to his feet and wiped the blade on a handkerchief.

"Two minutes and thirty-three seconds it took you to do it, Captain," announced the Britisher, snapping shut his watch. "But a minute ago I wouldn't have bet a penny candle on your life."

In fact the end had come so suddenly that the audience was stunned; it was only when they saw four Kroomen bearing the body of Guerra away that they realized the Sea Fox had made good his bluff.

As is always the case, the crowd was with the winner and the victor was immediately surrounded by a knot of captains eager to congratulate him.

"I ain't got no time to hold a palaver, gentlemen," said the Sea Fox, "ye will have to excuse me, but I've got a lot to do."

PAYING NO attention to the extended hands, he called Cha-cha and Captain Walters to one side.

"I wanta be under weigh by sundown," he told Cha-cha, "an' I wish you'd begin putting my slaves aboard."

"Come up to my office and we will talk it over," rejoined the mulatto, loath to see all this money escaping him.

"There ain't nothin' to talk over 'tall," retorted Cap'n Pepper, pulling a white handkerchief from the pocket of the coat he had just donned. "My second has a written agreement."

"Certainly," purred Cha-cha, "that part is all right; but I cannot begin putting your slaves aboard until tomorrow."

"An' give ye time to pick out all the good ones an' sub'stoot them winnowings ye got in your barracoon, eh? Howsomever, I was prepared for this."

The Sea Fox stepped to the water's edge and waved the handkerchief.

Almost instantly there came the clank of capstan pawls as

his crew hove taut on the spring and the grim muzzles of the *Wild Pigeon's* starboard battery began to frown toward the shore.

"Well done, Tom Dollar!" cried the Sea Fox.

Then, turning to Cha-cha, he fixed the mulatto with eyes that were terrible in their intensity.

"Ye see how my guns are trained, don't ye? Well, if the first canoe-load o' my slaves ain't on the way to my ship inside of twenty minutes I'll blow that gingerbread palace o'yours to hell an' ye with it—get that?"

"You win, Cap'n," said Cha-cha, yielding with good grace. "Your slaves will all be aboard by sundown. And, if ever you want a job as general manager for me at a salary that would stagger you, please come to me."

With the slaves moving rapidly to his ship the Sea Fox heaved a sigh and started on what he considered the worst job of all—to get Rosella and tell her that there would be no wedding. First he and the steward got the four girls whom Guerra had married and then cast-off; together they all went up to Rosella's. In twenty minutes these four had convinced the weeping girl that she had indeed had a fortunate escape.

"But where is Captain Guerra now?" she asked as, a little later, the Sea Fox put her in a canoe to go aboard.

"I don't know, Rosella," he answered gently. "Nobody knows where he's gone. An' that's no lie, either," he added under his breath.

As the last canoe-load of slaves left the shore and Cap'n Pepper was stepping into another canoe to go aboard, he was held up by a group of captains.

"We've sent you off a half-dozen cases of wine as a little token of our regard, Captain Pepper," their spokesman, the Britisher, informed him. "And we are wondering if you would mind telling us whether you originated that trick you used to get Guerra or did you learn it from someone?"

"Gentlemen," returned the Sea Fox earnestly. "I l'arned that trick from a better man than I ever will be, no other than Jim

Bowie himself. He give me that tip one night when him an' his brother Resin stopped overnight at my father's farm. I was a lad at the time. Well, the jug of applejack got to circulatin' pretty freely an' when the talk switched roun' to the subject o' duels, Jim got down on the kitchen floor an' showed us how he got a man once jest the same way as ye see me get Guerra today."

He stepped into the canoe.

"But," he added, "I wouldn't advise nobody to try it unless they was pretty sure o' their legs an' had practised some little bit on a dummy. Good-by, gentlemen, an' thank ye most heartily for yer present."

A CLOSE-REEFED HONOR

*Apparently it was only lubberly seamanship
that bumped the* **Peerless Ann** *into the* **Wild
Pigeon,** *but the wise old eyes of the Sea Fox
read in it a trick that threatened peril for
his crew and confiscation for his vessel*

"STARB'ARD YER helm. Hard a-starb'ard! Where the hell yer go-in', ye hake-headed son of a dogfish, ye?"

Having roared this out in a voice which easily carried from one bank of the Bonny River to the other, Tom Dollar, chief mate of the American slaver-brigantine *Wild Pigeon*, leaped on the port poop-rail quite regardless of the fierce West African sun shooting its burning rays mercilessly down on him. The mate, steadying himself with a hand on the t'gallant backstay, flung out a long arm and shook an immense bony fist at the skipper of another craft, which was being fanned along by a light breeze and which, if she held her course, most certainly would foul the *Wild Pigeon*.

As his practiced, apprehensive eyes made a sweeping appraisal alow and aloft of the oncoming vessel, Tom Dollar gave a snort of disgust. She was brigantine-rigged, of about the same tonnage as the slaver, and with something like the same lines. But her poor abused hull evidently had not been touched by a paint brush for many a long month. Her slovenly set sails were worn as thin as a poor-house sheet, and her standing rigging, hanging in bights, fairly screamed for an application of tar. She rejoiced in the name of the *Peerless Ann*, and Tom Dollar recognized her as an old wagon that had been lying on the mud flats of Old Calabar (Duke Town) for at least five years to his knowledge. Duke Ephraim, the king, had taken her over from a Portuguese slaver in payment of a bad debt and had allowed her to rot.

Her skipper, clad in a not over-clean suit of white duck, stood on the poop with his mate, a swarthy Portuguese. His long, lank frame somewhat resembled Tom Dollar's, but here all resemblance ended, for the slaver's nose was curved like a lobter's claw, whereas the stranger's was a regular wind-splitter of a nose, fashioned like a fore stays'l, and having a decided list to starboard. And his eyes of a beady shifting green, were quite unlike the frank gray eyes, fearless as the noon, of Tom Dollar.

After looking blandly in the direction of the incensed mate with a gaze which apparently swept past without seeing him, the captain of the *Peerless Ann* turned to his mate with an air of well simulated surprise.

"Blow me fer pickles, Manuel," he observed in a voice the high, thin tones of which carried it distinctly to the ears of Tom Dollar, " 'tain't possible that there sheer-legged, tumbled-down-lookin' clam-digger is addressin' me, is it? If I thought so, blow me if I wouldn't run alon'side an' use that hay-maker fer a toggle fer our fore bowlin'." He gave a shrill, cackling laugh.

"Hell's lifts! You'll find out who I'm a-talkin' to if ye foul my vessel!" roared back Tom Dollar. "I'll come aboard an' do a man's work on ye if ye touch my paint. I'll set up yer riggin' for ye all a-taunto if ye puckerrow with me."

"Can't understan' what that feller's a-ravin' 'bout, Manuel," continued the skipper of the *Peerless Ann,* still gazing over Tom Dollar's head. "But he ain't wantin' us, that's sartain. If he did he'd a-signaled us by hangin' that dirty red undershirt he's a-wearin' in the main riggin'."

A realization of the fact that among his extensive collection of profanely cutting phrases he had none adequate to fit this studied affront made Tom Dollar splutter and grind savagely on his quid, while his face turned nearly black with impotent rage. The Portuguese mate haw-hawed in great glee at his skipper's facetiousness, and the latter, quite well pleased with himself and still surveying some imaginary person or thing in the rear of Tom Dollar, signaled with his hand for the helmsman to put the wheel up.

The skipper had no intention of fouling the *Wild Pigeon*, though, from "the particular hell he raised generally" later on, Tom Dollar always swore that he did. On coming on deck with his mid-forenoon livener of a tumbler of Old Medford rum tingling soothingly under his belt, he had observed the *Wild Pigeon*, in which for reasons of his own he had more than a casual interest, and had accordingly run down to take a look at her.

CRASH! THE two vessels bumped together, owing to the stupidity of the frowsy, black-bearded beachcomber at the wheel, who misconstrued the signal and put the wheel the wrong way. There followed the ominous ripping of rotten cotton on the ancient vessel, and, her fore lift carrying away, her fore yard cockbilged in a dangerous manner but was quickly secured by some of her crew. No harm was done the slaver save fraying a little chafing gear and rubbing some paint from her bends, but Tom Dollar had not stopped to ascertain this. The moment the vessels clashed he made a flying leap for the skipper on the poop of the *Peerless Ann*. The latter sidestepped with wonderful alacrity, slammed a hard right at the slaver's jaw, missed, and Tom Dollar, carried on by his momentum, went sprawling to the deck.

Captain Zadok Sparks was about to bring his heavy boots into play and make a quick and decisive end to the affair by the method known as "stomping up one side and down the other" when he was seized by the neck in a grip of steel. Twisting his head around he looked up into the black, shining face of Robin Hood, the giant Negro bosun of the *Wild Pigeon.* The bosun at the same time had grabbed Manuel and began twisting his arm until the pistol the Portuguese was trying to use dropped to the deck. Robin Hood dexterously clutched the barrel between the toes of his left foot and, with a quick backward fling, sent the weapon spinning overboard.

"Yah jes' bettah let Mister Dollah get on his feet, sah," boomed the bosun to the skipper, "or I'se liable to forget what mah ole mammy tole me, 'bout allus bein' berry respectful to white folks, sah."

Whereupon Tom Dollar sprang to his feet and, bounding onto the main deck, invited the skipper down in no unmistakable language. Robin Hood released his hold of the skipper and in another moment the belligerents were swirling about the deck like two miniature whirlwinds merging into one. Some of the slaver's crew had followed their officers aboard the vessel to see fair play. The dozen or so beachcombers composing the crew of the *Peerless Ann* showed no disposition to interfere, however, but gathered in the waist, eagerly watching the fight.

The fur was flying merrily when a short, stocky man, as hard as a bollard, and seeming to sweat power at every pore, threw his five-foot-five figure over the rail from a canoe on the opposite side of the ship. At the sudden appearance of Cap'n Pepper, the Sea Fox, his men grinned and winked knowingly at one another.

Dropping lightly to the deck, the Sea Fox took in the situation with one lightning sweep of his piercing black eyes. His heavy shoulders shook a little, as if agitated by some emotion, at the spectacle of Tom Dollar seated astride and holding onto the ears of the prancing, rearing skipper, who was backing toward the pin-rail with the obvious intention of scraping off his rider as an angry bull does a hornet.

After scratching the end of his short, freckled nose and allowing his hand to slide down into his beard, as if rubbing off a laugh, the crag-like brows of the Sea Fox drew together in a frown as he stepped up to the combatants, his men making way for him deferentially.

"Mr. Dollar!" he roared, in a voice which coming from that barrel-like chest really resembled thunder. "What's this I see? You a-neglectin' of yer duties an' a-playin' horse here on another ship's deck like a ten-year old schoolboy. What d'ye mean by it? Get back aboard yer ship, sir. Where's the cappen of this here craft, anyway?"

At a sign from him, Robin Hood got in front of Tom Dollar, who had dismounted at the sight of his skipper, but still showed every inclination to renew the combat.

"I be!" snapped Captain Sparks mopping his streaming face with the sleeve of his torn shirt. "I be skipper. An' blow me fer pickles if this don't beat anythin' I ever see in all my born days. Here I be a-comin' quietly into port when the consarned current sots me up again' your vessel, an' the next thing I knows that cussed wildcat leaps aboard me, flat-footed an' all toes spread, an' tries to chaw me plumb up. Ain't that so, Manuel?" He appealed to his mate, who nodded a vigorous assent. "You darn New Yorkers," added Captain Sparks, "seem to think ye own the hull universe, but I can tell ye don't own Cape Cod nor me nuther."

Tom Dollar's prominent larynx pumped up and down indignantly and he was about to sputter his version of the affair when he was silenced by the Sea Fox, who suddenly threw out his left arm, palm down, at right angles to his body.

"Stop. I have something important to communicate. We are in imminent danger," the gesture signified.

"WAAL, WAAL, Capt'in," purred the Sea Fox, "I'm mighty sorry this thing occurred. I be, really. Accidents'll happen, an' I don't s'pose ye was to blame for it 'tall. You'll have to excuse my mate, though. He's so jealous of his paint he'd tackle an admiral if he marked it any. But sho', there don't seem to be no harm done to ships or men, so what d'ye say, Capt'in, if we let it go at that?"

"Blow me fer pickles," began Captain Sparks, feeling his reddened ears gingerly, "that sounds—"

"An'," continued the Sea Fox, "Mr. Dollar will take some o' his men an' help yer mate get his ship clear an' anchored in a good spot while ye come aboard my ship Capt'in, an' help me wind the chronometer. I got some o' the finest Old Medford ye ever see; ten year old, every drop on't."

At this announcement Captain Sparks' face brightened visibly, and whatever hesitation still lingered in his mind was overcome by the Sea Fox taking his arm. The next moment they were going over the rail together and boarding the *Wild Pigeon.*

"Cappen Pepper wouldn't even listen to our side o' it, did ye notice, Robin Hood," observed Tom Dollar, disgustedly squirting a stream of tobacco juice at a rooster which just then poked its head out between the slats of a nearby hen coop. "That means he's got use for that there Cape Codder. An' he give me the danger sign, too. The hull thing's a puzzle to me, Robin Hood; but in course it wouldn't be possible for us to come on the coast without settin' all hell a-poppin', looks like."

Tom Dollar had followed the two skippers with his eyes, and before Captain Sparks followed the Sea Fox down the companionway the former turned and looked at the slaver mate, his horse-like face hideous with enmity. Tom Dollar returned that menacing look by giving the signal known among seamen as "The International Thumb-nail Code"—the thumb-nail is placed rigidly against the tip of the nose while the remaining four digits are agitated vigorously from side to side in the direction of the signalee. Captain Sparks reserved his reply to this signal probably waiting for a more opportune occasion.

A line run ashore to a convenient tree on the river bank and then taken to the amid-ship capstan of the *Peerless Ann* warped her clear of the slaver, and, as soon as she had room to swing in, her killick was let go, the whole operation not consuming more than half an hour. Then Manuel, the Portuguese mate, not to be outdone in the matter of hospitality by the Sea Fox, invited Tom Dollar below to "help wind the chronometer."

An hour later Cap'n Pepper, returning aboard with Sparks, found Tom Dollar with his nose as red as a boiled lobster's claw and both mates talking at once.

Captain Sparks hastened to his state-room with a heavy bulge in the starboard pocket of his duck jacket and when he returned and joined them in the after cabin, Tom Dollar noticed that the bulge was gone. Still he was not a little surprised when the Sea Fox drew from his pocket a bill of sale wherein it was stated that the *Peerless Ann,* in consideration of the sum of $1,750 paid to Captain Zadok Sparks, had now become the property of Captain Barnabas N. Pepper, and the two mates were forthwith requested to sign the document as witnesses of this sudden proceeding. Then Captain Sparks, now all smiles, proposed that they all take another look at the chronometer and the bargain was sealed and delivered in the presence of four ship's glasses tilted at an alarming angle in the direction of the skylight.

The vessel was thus turned over to the new owner and in another half hour Captain Sparks and the white portion of his crew were on the way to the shore with their dunnage. The Sea Fox had retained the six krumen of Sparks' crew, informing them that from now on their wages were doubled; instead of four dollars they were to receive eight dollars a month. In consequence the joy of the krumen was unbounded, but it is safe to say that, had they known what the Sea Fox intended doing with the *Peerless Ann,* they would not have shipped with him for a corresponding amount of millions.

By the time Sparks and his men were waddling up the broad, black-mud street of Bonny the crew of the slaver was busy as bees about the hull and rigging of the *Peerless Ann.* Stages were slung over her sides and long-handled scrapers and paint brushes, wielded by hard-bitten sailors sweating out a double allowance of grog, scraped off the blisters and slapped on the paint. From aloft came the wailing cry of the riggers to hoist or slack away on the gantlines as the worn out sails were unbent and replaced by serviceable ones.

When the work was well under way and everything going like clockwork the Sea Fox called Tom Dollar to one side.

"I signaled ye a while back that I had sunthin' important to commun'cate, Tom Dollar. Waal, jedge for yerself," he said somberly. "Commodore Gregory is a-comin' up the coast, an' is due off the bar here by sundown if not before. How d'ye like that?"

"AT SUNDOWN! Gregory!" ejaculated Tom Dollar, his eyes suddenly protruding. "Hell's—hell's lifts!" He removed the quid from his mouth and with a trembling hand threw it into the river, the Sea Fox eyeing him narrowly, yet after the manner of one who is doing some deep thinking himself.

Tom Dollar bit off another chew, looked dazedly at the ragged end of the plug and returned it to his pocket.

"Gregory's got us jest where he had us two years ago," he blurted. "An' we can't 'scape through that creek between the Bonny an' the Andoni Rivers the way we did afore, nuther. He's onto that trick by this time, Cappen. But how'd ye l'arn all this?"

"I heard it ashore. Duke Ephraim sent me word from Calabar by one o' his spies. As soon's I heard about it I hurried off to tell ye an' I find ye scrappin' with Hell-fire Sparks, as he's called."

"Hell's lifts! He dee-liberate—"

"Another thing that 'pears mighty signif'cant," interrupted Cap'n Pepper, "is that this here Sparks was aboard the brig *Bainbridge*, Gregory's ship, in Calabar, ye know, for more'n an hour, an' arter leavin' her he hurries an' buys this basket off'n Duke Ephraim for five hundred dollars."

Tom Dollar started and stared hard at his skipper.

"Sink me, Cappen, but I can see through a block when the sheave's gone as well's the next one," he replied. "You're a-thinkin' that this Sparks is jest a tool o' the commodore's. In short, that Gregory is a-settin' a trap for the Fox."

"Eggs-actly, Tom Dollar. Now brail out yer ears an' listen. In the fust place, Gregory palavers for over an hour with this here Sparks, one o' the greatest rascals on the coast. He used to have a tradin' station at Akassa Creek, on the Brass River, but he cheated so the native traders combined an' shut the trade on him. Waal, Gregory ain't havin' no truck with that kind o' man 'less he's a-goin' to use him, savvy? In the second place, why does a close-mouthed man like Gregory let everybody know where he's bound for when he leaves Old Calabar? He might jest as well sent me word hisself that he was a-comin'.

"I'll tell ye, Tom Dollar, he knows I'm here and he wants me to see part o' the cards he's a-playin'! Ye remember him an' me played a game right here two years ago an' I won by a hair. At that if he'd been mean 'nough to a-broke his word he could 'a' got me. Ye know that?"

The mate nodded and knit his brows in a puzzled frown.

"Hell's lifts, Cappen, this here is gettin' too damn' thick fur me, as the parrot said when he falls into the tar-barrel. What's Gregory up to, anyway? How's he calculate on gettin' ye?"

"Waal, I've figgered it out this way, Tom Dollar. Gregory has Sparks buy the *Peerless Ann* an' sends him up here ahead, figgerin' that when I hear he's a-comin' I'll buy the brigantine an' use her for a decoy. Send her out ahead, ye know, an' while Gregory is chasin' her slip out with the *Wild Pigeon* an' away."

The mate flung his head back, his mouth popping open in amazement.

"An' ye does that same thing, plays right into his hands," snorted he. Hell's lifts, why don't ye hand him over the *Wild Pigeon* an' done with it. There's only one way outa this, Cappen, an' that is up killick, pile the canvas on the *Wild Pigeon,* an' get outa here before the *Bainbridge* heaves in sight."

"An' leave my five hundred and forty-nine niggers I got ashore there in the barracoon as a present for King Dappa, eh?" barked the Sea Fox. "That 'ud be a hell of a way to treat Calvin Gale, our owner, wouldn't it? If I did that, Tom Dollar, I'd be too 'shamed to ever show my face in the Astor Bar ag'in. But rest easy. I'm a-goin' to let Gregory take the fust couple o' tricks an' welcome. There's jest one thing puzzles me, though. I'm pretty sure that Gregory knows that I'm onto his play an' the whole thing simmers down now to the way we handle the decoy. Does Gregory figger on me loadin' my slaves onto the decoy an' reshipping them aboard the *Wild Pigeon* at sea, or does he figger on me takin' the ord'nary course, runnin' the decoy out loaded with sand and then bring my slaves out on the *Wild Pigeon* when the coast is clear? I'm damned if I know, an' there ain't no way to find out."

He thought a long moment.

"Whatever Gregory has made up his mind to do I see I got to fix things so'll he chase the decoy," he added, glancing at his watch. "It's three o'clock now. I'm a-goin' down to the lookout station at Field Point an' watch my friend Gregory come in. Keep on with the work, Tom Dollar, an' when you're finished here heave short on the chain an' then do the same on the *Wild Pigeon.* The tide turns at midnight an' if there's any wind both these hooker's are a-goin' to sea, Gregory or no Gregory."

As he was getting into the dingy he added, as a thought struck him, "If that Sparks comes 'round, don't let him aboard either vessel. He may have it in for ye for the way ye rode him an' try to get back at ye, though I expect he's drunk by this time. But jest the same don't have no truck with him in any case. I'll be back soon's I get the lay o' things an' give ye a hand."

EIGHTY FEET in the air on the lookout platform in the top of an immense cotton tree Pepper looked down through a powerful glass onto the deck of the American brig-of-war *Bainbridge* as, a half hour before sunset, she came sweeping in and dropped anchor in eleven fathoms of water about a quarter of a mile distant from the high bluff of Field Point. As the Sea Fox had feared, some of her boat davits were empty and apparently a large part of her crew were absent. This signified that Gregory was aware that the Sea Fox was in the river and had dispatched a boating expedition up the Adoni River to prevent his escape by that channel. There was nothing left for the *Wild Pigeon* to do but try to run the blockade.

Despite the present shortage of hands aboard the man-of-war everything about her breathed a spirit of perfect order and discipline. Her decks were snow white; her guns shone like mirrors in the slanting flood of light from the declining sun, and the yards were squared by lifts and braces to a hair. But the Sea Fox, chewing vigorously on his inevitable quill toothpick, naturally was in no mood to appreciate this show of efficiency, which he well knew was not confined merely to keeping the ship in nautical perfection—as the many captures of slavers by Gregory and his squadron could testify. Yes, indeed, the slaver knew well the caliber of the tall, alert man in a white and gold uniform he could see standing there on her quarter conversing with two of his officers.

The Sea Fox sighed. Less than two years ago he and Gregory had fought side by side on the bloody deck of a Portuguese slaver; he to recover the slaves the Portuguese had stolen from him, and Gregory to take her as a prize. At the risk of his own life he had saved Gregory and over two hundred slaves from being blown up on that same vessel. He liked and admired the commodore immensely and he knew that personally Gregory had an equal regard for him. He also knew that the stern nature of the business on which the navy man was now engaged allowed no room for sentiment. Gregory would lay him by the heels if he possibly could, and the Sea Fox was the last man to blame one for doing one's duty.

"Waal, Commodore," commented the Sea Fox, half aloud, as he slung the glass over his shoulder preparatory to descending to the ground, "you've the same as challenged me to match wits with ye, an' I accept it. I ain't sayin' I'm any smarter than you be, for I ain't. But I've had twenty years' experience in this business an' I'm a-goin' to stake that ag'in' yer guns an' men. An', Commodore, you're a-goin' to be a mighty busy man afore mornin' and that's a fact."

THAT WEDNESDAY morning at one o'clock both vessels were ready for sea, their sails loosed and hanging in the gear ready for setting. The Sea Fox saw the last of his slaves safely under the *Wild Pigeon's* hatches and then, taking a last look alow and aloft in the bright moonlight at his beloved vessel, he gave Tom Dollar his final instructions.

"You'll have to take the ship home, Tom Dollar, the same's ye did three years ago," he ordered. "I'll follow as soon's as I can in one o' those Salem traders anchored along the Bight. Robin Hood is on lookout at Field Point an' he'll let go a rocket the minute there's a chance for ye to get clear. He'll be waiting for ye in a canoe abreast the point an' catch ye as you go by. You've got a fair wind an' tide, so set stuns'l alow an' aloft soon's yer anchor leaves the bottom. An' remember, Tom Dollar, stop for nothin' an' drive the old gal, drive her like hell. There ain't no keel in these waters can touch ye. That's all."

They shook hands and the stocky little skipper got into his dingy and pulled over to the *Peerless Ann*, now down to her loading mark with a hold half full of sand. Twenty minutes later, under all plain sail, before a brisk east southeast breeze, she was slipping by the dark mangrove bank on the port side.

Besides his six krumen the Sea Fox had picked two of his men, Sullivan and Avery—one time bucko mates of the Black

Ball Line—from the *Wild Pigeon* and placed them in charge of the krumen. He had told the ex-mates of the daring enterprise he was about to engage in, but they went about the decks seeing that everything was shipshape and the gear ready for running as coolly as if they were merely bound on an excursion down Long Island Sound.

"By ole Neptune's houn' pup," chuckled the Sea Fox, who was at the wheel, "this ole hooker ain't so bad. She can sail anyway." To his men he added, "Check them starb'ard braces in a p'int."

Soon they were passing Field Point with the sea cresting on the bar. In plain sight and a little farther out the black bulk of the *Bainbridge* bowed to the glittering swell.

Gregory had lookouts at both mastheads and the *Peerless Ann* had been reported at least two minutes before she flashed round the Point. The *Bainbridge* at once hauled on the spring she had to her cable so that nine long, protruding muzzles covered the approach of the daring slaver. The latter was holding a course which would force her to pass within biscuit toss of the man-of-war and just then, to the commodore's unspeakable amazement, he made out the unmistakable figure of the Sea Fox standing calmly at the wheel. At the same time the breeze bore to the navy man's nostrils a sickening, fetid odor like that emanating from the bodies of sweating Negroes closely confined.

"Great Jupiter! Mr. Plummer," he sang out hurriedly to his first lieutenant, "she is loaded to the deck-beams with slaves."

A gun was then fired, sending a shot across the bows of the *Peerless Ann,* while in a twinkling the yards of the *Bainbridge* were clothed with canvas as the sails were hoisted and sheeted home. Gregory leaped on the quarter-rail and hailed the oncoming vessel, now not more than a hundred feet away.

"Heave-to, Captain Pepper," he roared through his trumpet, "or I shall be forced to sink you!"

"How de do, Commodore. How air ye? Fine night fer a sail,

ain't it?" came back the answer from what looked, in the mellow moonlight like a statue of bronze standing at the wheel.

"Don't be a damn' fool, Pepper," snapped the commodore. "You're making it mighty hard for me, but if you don't heave-to, by the gods. I'll blow you out of water."

This time he received no reply, unless the setting of the port topmast stuns'l aboard the *Peerless Ann* could be considered as such.

"Fire!" bellowed the commodore, leaping from the rail. "Let him have it. He is asking for it."

Three of the after guns of the port battery, the only ones that would bear at that moment, boomed and every shot told. One struck the forward part of the house close to where Sullivan was standing, rending off great splinters, one of which drove clear through the ex-mate's body, protruding a foot from his breast. He staggered back for several feet and then fell in a huddled heap to the deck. Another shot went through the galley, just missing the galley stove and plumped into the sea a hundred yards away. The third shot tore through the bulwarks from side to side and went to join its companion in the sea.

Captain Pepper ground away on his toothpick. Observing that the man-of-war had slipped her cable and was wearing round in pursuit, he braced in his yards, keeping off so that the *Bainbridge* could only use her bow-chasers, and at the same time trying to lead the navy brig onto the Rama Bank, which had only about eleven feet of water on it in some places. The Sea Fox bumped the *Peerless Ann* across it and saw twenty feet of her rotten keel swirl up in her wake in consequence.

The *Bainbridge* refused to enter the trap, however, but bore up and gave him a full broadside, some of the shots of which passed clear through the brigantine's poor hull, but none, fortunately, injured her top-hamper. Looking back at the river mouth, now six miles away, Captain Pepper could just discern the *Wild Pigeon* as she crossed the bar and flew like a frightened thing to the northwest. Whereupon the Sea Fox hauled his wind and kept well to the southward, the shots from the *Bainbridge's* long thirty-two's kicking up the water all about him.

From the time the Sea Fox drove the *Peerless Ann* across the Bonny bar he had no chance of escaping, and he knew it. But he was determined to give Gregory a run for his money, and so it was quite sun-up before a well directed shot brought joy to the heart of Gregory as he saw the brigantine's fore-topmast go by the board.

"A good job, too," commented the Sea Fox to his men. "There's twelve feet o' water in her hold now an' she's drinkin' in the rest o' the ocean as fast's she can. She'll go down in another ten minutes. Lower away the boat."

And sink she did, within the time specified, to the intense dismay and chagrin of Gregory, who, as his vessel approached, saw the *Peerless Ann* suddenly elevate her stern high in the air and plunge out of sight, bowsprit first, into the depths.

With her going Gregory realized that all his planning and all his labor had been in vain. The evidence against the Sea Fox was a thousand fathoms down. He had nothing now on which to hold the slaver.

So as the Sea Fox boarded the man-of-war a few minutes later he was met at the gangway by Gregory, his resolute clean shaven face shadowed by a look of unwonted sternness.

"I never expected to see you go that far, Captain Pepper," he stated tensely. "Is it possible that you are the same man who once showed his willingness to sacrifice his own life to save me and two hundred slaves from sudden death?" He stopped and looked sorrowfully at the little captain.

"I dunno, Commodore," replied the Sea Fox. "Except p'raps I'm a leetle more bald, I guess I'm about the same."

"This is no time for jesting, sir," Gregory turned on him savagely. "Tell me how many human beings went down on that ship?"

"One. One o' my men killed by a splinter. The rest o' my crew is all here, sir!"

"One!" repeated the commodore, incredulously. "You mean to say that there were no slaves on that vessel when she sank?"

"Nary a one, Commodore." The Sea Fox turned and waved his hand in a northwesterly direction. "My slaves is all aboard the *Wild Pigeon* off there somewhere. If it wasn't so hazy you'd be able to see her yet. She crossed the bar 'bout a hour an' a half ago. Ye was probably so busy a-chasin' me ye didn't notice her."

The brows of the commodore bent in a puzzled frown.

"But, Captain, I tell you I smelled them," he declared. "If that stench didn't come from Negroes then my nose needs overhauling sadly."

"Yer smellers is all right, sir," Cap'n Pepper grinned. "That there smell would fool anybody, I guess. But 'twan't nuthin' but a bucket o' beef-bones an' some rancid fat a-burnin' in my galley-stove. If that smell hadn't fooled ye you'd 'a' got me sure as shootin'. You'd 'a' let me pass an' caught the *Wild Pigeon* as she came out." He shot a quick, penetrating glance at the navy man. "Ain't that the way ye figgered when ye got Sparks to come up here on that old wagon from Calabar, Commodore?" he added quietly.

"It doesn't matter now how I figured," returned Gregory despondently. Then his sense of humor taking the ascendant, he burst into a laugh. "Tricked, by George! Tricked by a bucket of beef-bones! The drinks are on me, Captain Pepper."

Then to the unbounded astonishment of the ship's company, who were not aware of the singular circumstances which linked these two men, the commodore tucked his arm into the Sea Fox's and led him below. They had hardly left the deck when the lookout at the masthead sang out, "Sa-aa-il ho-o-o!"

GREGORY AND the Sea Fox immediately went on deck again. The mist to the southward and westward which had hitherto concealed the strange sail had now been mopped up by the sun and Gregory at once went aloft to the masthead. The breeze which had been gradually lessening for the last hour now died out altogether, the great topsails of the brig slatting with the lift of the sea with a violence enough to make a sail-maker weep.

"A Spanish schooner and full to the gunwales with slaves," reported the commodore as he presently descended to the deck. "It is old Marcellino. His fore topmast is a couple of fathoms longer than the main, the only vessel rigged that way on this coast or anywhere else, I guess."

"Once, Captain Pepper, you gave me the pleasure of chasing a slaver in your vessel." He smiled at the Sea Fox. "Now if I had a capful of wind I would give you the same sport, and believe me it would be no empty honor to capture old Marcellino; he is nearly as clever as yourself. Whistle and pray for a wind, everybody."

The steward came to announce that breakfast was ready. At the table Gregory and the Sea Fox were joined by the surgeon and the purser. The latter two, who were acquainted with the manner in which the Sea Fox had once saved the commodore's life, were very courteous and friendly to the slaver. The commodore, however, took little part in the conversation, appearing most of the time in a deep study, which fact the Sea Fox could not help observing.

After the meal the four adjourned to the quarter-deck. There they could see the bluish line of the coast astern, and off the port beam, seven miles away on the glassy sea, two little patches of shimmering white—the topsails of the slave-schooner.

Commodore Gregory did not seat himself, like the others, in the shade of the spanker, but paced back and forth with long, nervous strides, squinting at the tempting prize and biting his lips and at times surveying the Sea Fox in a very thoughtful manner indeed.

"The Old Man is fairly sweating under the collar," observed the purser in a low tone. "A slaver, to the commodore, is like a red rag to a bull."

"Damn the calm!" burst out the young surgeon. "A good, stiff breeze now might give us that prize-money we thought we were going to handle through your capture, Captain Pepper."

The latter grinned and twirled his toothpick, quite satisfied with things as they were—for was not his ship safely away on the high seas with a cargo that would bring the owner at least one hundred and fifty thousand dollars profit.

"By George! I'll do it," suddenly exclaimed Gregory, to no one in particular. "I've made up my mind. I'm deuced if Marcellino is going to stump me this way." Whereupon he made three strides to the skylight and called down for the steward to tell Mr. Plummer he wanted him.

The first lieutenant hurried on deck and Gregory, taking him to one side, conversed with him eagerly for perhaps three minutes, both of them every now and then casting side-glances at the Sea Fox seated unconcernedly in a deck-chair. Finally the lieutenant nodded and with a broad grin on his bronzed features went to the waist and gave an order to the bosun, who forthwith put a shining whistle to his lips and piped all hands.

Gregory then came back to the three men on the quarter-deck.

"My launch and first cutter are away up the Adoni River blocking the creek that our friend here escaped through two years ago," he said. "Now I've just men enough left to man the remaining cutter and the gig. Mr. Plummer will take ten sailors and two marines in the launch—it carries a four-pound swivel—and I'll take the gig with the remaining six sailors and four marines, and we shall pull over and take that fellow by boarding. He's probably laughing up his sleeve now, but we may change his tune inside of two hours. I'm leaving you in charge here, Captain Pepper, until I return,"

"What?" shouted the Sea Fox, leaping from his seat, scarcely able to credit his own ears. "What's that ye say, Commodore? Ye want me to take charge of this hooker till ye get back?"

"Exactly. Why not? There isn't a man in the seven seas in whom I have more confidence. With your seven men and the purser, surgeon, cook and steward, you can handle her easily. If you get any wind you can work the ship up to us."

"Come on, Captain Pepper, say the word," put in the bluff lieutenant, coming up. "We've got to stir our stumps to get alongside that fellow before he catches a breeze. Every minute is precious."

Cap'n Pepper gasped helplessly as he looked at the commodore and then at the man-of-war jacks crowding aft, their faces glowing with excitement at the idea of a chase, and every eye fixed with inquiring eagerness upon him.

Comprehending that, as the Sea Fox was himself a slaver, the ethics of the case were probably the cause of his hesitation, Gregory pointed out that he was considered a neutral and that all he was expected to do was to manage the ship.

"Oh, I know it's what ye call a close-reefed honor you're a-handin' me," rejoined the Sea Fox, "but—" hearing an impatient murmur from the man-of-war's men— "Jumpin' Jehu, all right, Commodore, go to it! I owe ye a good turn, anyway. I'll take charge here till ye get back."

The crew gave a rousing cheer as they heard his decision, and armed with muskets, pistols and cutlasses the men got into the boats and pushed off, in high glee not only at the prospect of gaining a nice bit of prize-money but also at the idea of having pressed the renowned slaver into their service.

"By the great Noah's buoy-rope, if this don't beat all I ever seen or hearn tell on in all my born days," the Sea Fox murmured into his beard, as with the surgeon and purser he stood by the quarter rail watching the rapidly receding boats. "I see now how Gregory gets things done," he told them. "Who could play a man dirty arter he trusts ye this way, I wanta know?"

Soon the boats were mere specks in the heat haze which the fiery sun seemed to draw from the smooth, glowing bosom of the sea. Then as the specks faded from his sight the Sea Fox went to the main masthead to follow the boats' movements through a powerful glass. He saw the boats, looking the size of ants at that distance, approach the schooner. Then came a deep boom as the slaver fired an eighteen pounder warning them away.

Followed the faint rattle of musketry, like someone hammering on an anvil afar off. The current was sweeping the *Bainbridge* rapidly inshore and there was that stagnant, deceptive morning vapor still lingering in places and obscuring part of the coast-line and reaching well out to sea to the north and westward. In fact, had the slaver-schooner been a few miles farther north she would have been concealed in this vapor and probably could have gone on her way undetected.

But all hands on the man-of-war were too busy straining their eyes and ears toward the scene of the conflict which was taking place just below the horizon to the southwest to pay attention to any natural phenomena or anything else for that matter, until the Sea Fox, hearing the sound of paddles alongside, looked down. Then, stern stuff as he was made of, he felt his legs turning to water, and his eyebrows jerked upward with a suddenness that sent bright specks floating before his eyes.

Rubbing his eyes with a convulsive movement, the Sea Fox looked down again. Yes, there was really a canoe alongside the gangway with five of his men in it, and, yes—yes, it was too true—there was Robin Hood and Tom Dollar, his two officers, whom he had supposed at least thirty miles at sea in charge of the *Wild Pigeon,* now climbing over the hammock-nettings.

CAP'N PEPPER allowed one gulping groan to escape his lips; then with a stoical shrug of his thick shoulders, and with his weather-beaten features as if turned to granite, he slung the glass over his shoulder and descended the rigging. Tom Dollar, a bloody bandage about his head, his red flannel undershirt, half torn from his back, looked at him glassily as the Sea Fox swung from the sheerpole to the deck, then clutched blindly at the main clew-garnet, missed it and fell at the feet of his skip-per in a dead faint.

The surgeon and the purser had advanced toward them, but the surgeon, seeing this, ran down into the cabin and speedily returned with a bottle of brandy and a glass which he poured nearly full and handed to the slaver. Cap'n Pepper supported the mate's head on his knee and allowed a little of the liquor to trickle into the wounded man's mouth. At the very first swallow

Tom Dollar opened his eyes, sputtered, and, seizing the glass, drained it with infinite gusto.

"Hell's lifts! 'Tain't possible I went over like a young gal at the sight o' a sarpint, is it?" he inquired, looking about. "Fust time I ever done it in my life. I must be gettin' old."

"Mistah Dollah gottem bery bad cut on um head, sah," explained Robin Hood. "An' de wedder bery hot, sah."

"I'm as right as a trivet now," declared Tom Dollar, staggering to his feet. "Gimme—"

"Sot right down there in the shade with yer back ag'in' that gun-carriage, Tom Dollar," advised the Sea Fox. "There, that's right. D'ye think another drink would hurt him, Surgeon?"

"I wouldn't advise too much until I can have a look at that cut," returned the latter.

"Hell's lifts!" expostulated the mate. "That there one went down the port side. Give me a second drink for the other wing so's I'll be on a even keel like an' I'll tell ye what happened."

He was given another stiff drink and at a sign from the surgeon the bottle was emptied among the five foremast hands who had been in the canoe.

" 'Twas this way, Cappen," began Tom Dollar. "The hull thing's short an' sweet like an admiral's duff. I got the signal from Robin Hood as agreed on an' started to get my anchor—I was already hove short, ye remember. Waal 'bout then ole Chief Bottle Nose comes aboard with a lot o' his niggers an' says that King Dappa sends him for to help us get under way. This seems all accordin' to Gunter to me, seein's they had done that for us afore. But afore I knows it the hull deck is jest flooded with niggers an' they was so many on the windlass-brakes I takes a heaver an' clears some o' 'em away. This seems to be a sorter signal, for just then they is joined by that cussed Sparks an' his mate an' all them beachcombers he brings from Calabar with him.

"They was all a-flourishin' cutlasses an' made for us like they was a-goin' to mince us right there. Waal, we didn't have a damn' thing to fight with; only a few o' us could grab a handspike. I got one, though, an' was up on the starboard rail abaft the fore riggin' a-bustin' them niggers' haids like ripe gourds when Sparks swings into the riggin' alongside me afore I sees him an' gives me a swingdingin' swipe with his cutlass athwartships o' my skull. I tumbled clean overboard. Five of our men was already in a canoe—they had to jump over the side or be killed—an' they fished me outa water. The rest o' our men, I cal'late, was driv' below in the fo'cas'le an' the scuttle fastened over 'em.

"Waal, me an' my five men paddles ashore to Bonny an' by that time Sparks had the *Wild Pigeon* under way an' bound down the river. I goes to find King Dappa for to get him to send one o' his war canoes through the slue and cut off Sparks at Field Point. But, hell's lifts, Dappa was so drunk I couldn't make him savvy nothin' an' none o' his chiefs wouldn't dare start nothin' without his permission, for if they did he was liable to brain 'em as soon's he waked up. So we follers down-river in the canoe an' picks up Robin Hood, who nat'rally is all het up at bein' left behind, not knowin' as how the ship has changed han's. We doesn't know that you're aboard here exactly, Cappen, but we was a-goin' to try an' get the man-o-war to go arter Sparks, knowin' as how you'd rather see the *Wild Pigeon* blowed outa water than have that black-souled cuss get clear away with her. That's all. Thank ye, sir." This to the surgeon, who all the while had been deftly dressing the cut.

THE SEA FOX turned his head and stared dumbly toward the northwest, as if he were trying to pierce the haze, annihilate distance, and take one last look at his beautiful *Wild Pigeon*.

"I was so busy with the lion in the open I had no time to watch the jackals in the jungles," he observed huskily. "Not that I didn't consider 'em, though. I knowed Sparks would get back at ye if he could, Tom Dollar, and I also knowed he'd have no trouble gettin' that treach'rous Bottle Nose to help him for some o' that gold I paid him. But King Dappa told me hisself, an' I believe he acted in good faith, that Bottle Nose was one hundred and fifty miles up in the interior after slaves, somewheres round Diapan. Waal, King Dappa was mistook an' I pay in cons'quence. 'Tain't the fust time I've had to, but 'twas never quite so bad's this. Waal, we'll start all over ag'in an' that's all there is to it." He shrugged his shoulders and tugged at his beard a moment.

"Robin Hood, you jump aloft an' see-how our friend the commodore is a-makin' out," he then said briskly. "I ain't heard no guns lately. An' take a squint to the nor'west. Might be possible that the *Wild Pigeon* ain't off'n soundings yet. She couldn't 'a' been very far off shore when this ca'm shut down."

"Now let's see, Tom Dollar," Cap'n Pepper continued musingly, as Robin Hood sprang into the main rigging. "Sparks would never think o' takin' them slaves to the States, for he could never land 'em an' he knows it. He could find a market for 'em in Havana, but he owes every dealer round them parts so he won't go there, 'tain't likely. The nearest place an' the very man to deal with an' pay ready cash would be Cha-cha at Ayudah. An' there's where Sparks'll make for or I'll miss my guess. By the powers of Tophet—an' that's a red-hot oath, Tom Dollar—here comes a breeze!"

Almost at the same moment Robin Hood hailed the deck.

"I see him h'ist um 'Merican flag on schooner, sah!" he shouted down.

"Jumpin' Jehu! Hooraw for Gregory!" crowed the Sea Fox, his face shining. "He's one feller didn't make no mistake that time, Tom Dollar. Aloft there! See anythin' o' the *Wild Pigeon?*"

"No, sah. No see um yet, Cap'en. But haze luftin', sah. Mebbe see um bery soon, sah."

"A hundred dollars gold for ye if ye do, Robin Hood!" roared back the Sea Fox.

They were bracing round the yards to run down to Gregory when Robin Hood, with a queer catch in his voice, sent down news that sent a shiver of delight through those on deck.

"*Wild Pigeon* two p'ints on the starb'ard bow, sah. Um 'bout t'ree miles 'way sah!"

"Hooroo!" shouted Tom Dollar. "An' hooroo ag'in! I'll give another hundred, Robin Hood, if I can lay my grapplin'hooks on Sparks."

"Good 'nough, Tom Dollar," grinned Cap'n Pepper. "We'll catch our fish afore we eat 'em though. Brace up forrad sharp on the starb'ard tack an'board yer fore tack an'sheet. I'll tend to the main. Port main braces here, the rest o'ye!"

The *Bainbridge* had no sooner hauled her wind than Robin Hood reported that the ship ahead was acting very queerly. She had worn completely round and now seemed to be hanging in irons.

"Trouble aboard her," conjectured the Sea Fox. "Looks like Sparks has bitten off a little more'n he can chew. Either our men has busted outa the fo'cas'le an'taken charge or more likely them beachcombers has got scared at seein' a man-o'-war comin' for 'em an'has mutinied. Probably they're afraid that if they run an' get caught they'll be classed as pirates, which they be anyway."

Cap'n Pepper then went aloft to the masthead and remained about ten minutes, during which time the *Wild Pigeon* made no attempt to escape but lay nearly stationary on the water, her fore yards back.

"Yaas, Tom Dollar, there's somethin' queer goin' on aboard her, but the way she lays I couldn't see what 'twas," Cap'n Pepper remarked, as he and Robin Hood came down on deck. "Where the hell did ye git them clo'es?" noticing that the mate was wearing a petty-officer's jacket an' trousers.

Tom Dollar explained that the purser, seeing that his clothes were in ruins, had given them to him. This gave Cap'n Pepper an idea and he persuaded the purser to rig out his six white men in man-of-war uniforms, the sight of which he believed would have a great moral effect on Sparks and his men. By the time all this was done the *Bainbridge* was within a half mile of the *Wild Pigeon* and Tom Dollar trained a thirty-two pounder bow-chaser and sent a shot skipping across her bows "jest as a hint for 'em to keep quiet till we come up," as he expressed it. But to their astonishment it had just a contrary effect; the brigantine suddenly checked in her yards, eased her main sheet and, taking the wind just forward of the beam, began slipping through the water.

"Jumpin' Jehu!" exploded the Sea Fox in dismay. "We can never overhaul him now, Tom Dollar. That shows he never hove-to of his own accord. He must a-got his crew in subjection ag'in. Great Lord, look—look what the black-hearted devil is up to will ye!"

RIGHT BEFORE their horror-stricken eyes, all aboard the man-of-war, saw Sparks and his mate dragging a shackled slave aft along the poop. They lifted him up in plain sight on the rail, held him there a long moment to give their pursuers a good look, and then threw the black, squirming body overboard. It floundered, bobbing on the waves a minute or two. Then nothing could be seen but the closely shaven head rising and falling and now and then the manacled hands lifted in an imploring manner toward the oncoming man-of-war.

"He's done that to gain time," the Sea Fox explained to the purser and surgeon. "He reckons on us heavin' to an' pickin' up the poor feller."

"Which of course you will," assumed the surgeon.

"Which in course I won't!" blazed the Sea Fox, grimly. "Ye ferget, Surgeon, that Gregory took all the boats. An' my men what came alongside in the canoe let it go adrift."

He measured the distance between the two vessels with his eye and then ordered Tom Dollar to throw a shot close alongside the chase.

"If that don't stop 'em we'll take the spars outa her next," he added, his face taking on a look of fixed resolve. "I'd rather Gregory had her a million times than let Sparks get away."

The big port bow-chaser flamed and roared, and the heavy shot plumped so close to the starboard gangway of the *Wild Pigeon* that the spray of it dashed over her rail.

"Now that's what I call placing them!" exclaimed the purser admiringly. "And he's taking notice of it, too. Look!"

The fore lower and fore topsail yard flew suddenly aback and the *Wild Pigeon* came staggering up into the wind.

"Hell's lifts! Somebody aboard there cut the braces," jubilated Tom Dollar. "She's our meat now."

The wind had increased and the *Bainbridge* was soon within a cable's length of the slaver. Then by concerted arrangement the Sea Fox took the wheel while the purser, in his natty white uniform, paced the quarter, impersonating a navy captain. The last touch being given to naval picture by a man in the uniform of a Jacktar hoisting the Stars and Stripes to the peak of the *Bainbridge.*

The Sea Fox kept on until he had the weather gage of the *Wild Pigeon* and then with only about a hundred feet of water between the vessels he backed his fore yard and way was stopped on the *Bainbridge.*

At this juncture a heavily built, black-bearded beachcomber jumped on the starboard rail amidships.

"Cruiser, ahoy, there!" he hailed the man-of-war.

"Ahoy the brigantine!" rejoined the purser, throwing out his chest.

"For Gawd's sake, Cap'n, send some men aboard an' take this bloody, drunken skipper of ourn prisoner. We didn't have no hand in throwin' that nigger overboard. We—" He stopped short at seeing Sparks and Manuel the mate, emerging from the cabin where they had been nipping up their courage to meet this emergency with a huge potation of rum.

Sparks was bare-headed, his lank, black locks stringing about his ears. His right hand gripped the brass handle of a heavy, shining cutlass. He glared wildly at the cruiser; then, leering venomously at the beachcomber, he jerked a pistol from his belt and fired. The man on the rail flung both arms in the air and gave a convulsive spring overboard, shot through the heart.

"Yaas, damn yer souls, come aboard—come aboard an' git

me!" raved Sparks, dancing along the poop-rail and making his cutlass sing in the air. "Blow me fur pickles ef I can't lick any half dozen men ye got aboard that cockroach trap."

"Si, come aboard!" shrilled Manuel, full of alcoholic courage, and also flourishing his cutlass.

Tom Dollar and Robin Hood, armed with cutlasses, stood ready by the rail just forward of the port main rigging. The mate signaled with his hand to the Sea Fox at the wheel. The latter nodded to the men stationed at the braces, who immediately hauled the yards sharp against the starboard backstay. In another minute, so gently that she would have hardly crushed an egg-shell, the *Bainbridge's* port amid-ship-rail rocked against the weather counter of the slaver.

Robin Hood with one tremendous leap bounded clear over the head of Manuel, who turned partly round in a confused manner to fall the next instant cloven to the chin.

"There goes one o' 'em, Surgeon," chuckled the Sea Fox. "Sparks'll be the next."

As Tom Dollar landed lightly on the poop of the slaver Sparks made a rush at him, the skipper's face lighting up with a fierce, unholy joy as he recognized his old enemy.

"Ho-ho-ho," he jeered. "Ef here ain't the clam-digger ag'in. Ho-ho-ho!" Like a bolt of fury he threw himself on the mate, his cutlass flashing wickedly in the blazing sun.

"By the Jumpin' Jehu! Surgeon, now you're a-goin' to see sunthin' really pretty," the Sea Fox promised. "Robin Hood is good, but he ain't nuthin' compared to Tom Dollar."

"You shouldn't have allowed him to go," expostulated the surgeon. "He stands a fair chance of bursting those stitches I took in his head and reopening that wound."

"Don't ye bother none 'bout my mate, Surgeon," replied Cap'n Pepper. "His head won't bother him none. He can write his name on a feller with that cutlass o' hisn'n. Watch now."

The combatants were surging back and forth across the poop and Sparks seemed surrounded by a wall of flaming, clashing steel so rapidly did Tom Dollar parry and cut. They had not been engaged much over two minutes when the end came so quickly that no one looking on saw exactly how it happened. Sparks apparently was holding his own in fine shape when, of a sudden, Tom Dollar was seen to lean a little sidewise; his arm merely seemed to stiffen a little, yet Sparks sprawled to the deck, the two carotid arteries spouting like a ruptured garden-hose from his partly severed neck.

Robin Hood, with a face like a black, avenging god, picked up the body of Sparks in one hand and Manuel in the other and dumped them overboard, while Tom Dollar, panting a little, leaned against the skylight, cleaning the blade of his weapon with one of the binnacle rags.

Turning the wheel over to one of his men, the Sea Fox came to the quarter-rail.

"All you men that belonged to Sparks stir yer stumps an' get ready to come aboard here!" he roared. "Robin Hood, open that fo'cas'le scuttle an' let our men out, then get the whaleboat into the water an' bring all them pirates over here."

IN LESS than fifteen minutes eleven dejected, apprehensive looking men were going over the gangway of the *Bainbridge,* where they were handcuffed and lined up in the starboard waist. And a thoroughly frightened body of men they were at the idea of being prisoners on one of Uncle Sam's men-of-war, their alarm reaching the highest pitch upon the purser's pointing, with a ferocious scowl, at the fore yard-arm.

In answer to the Sea Fox's rapid questioning they avowed that they had thought it nothing but a good joke to loot a slaver, who was himself an outlaw. But that when they had seen a man-of-war in chase of them they had refused to work the vessel for Sparks but had attempted themselves to bring her nearer the man-of-war. Sparks and his mate, after threatening to shoot them, had finally braced the yards and attempted to escape. But they, watching their chance, had cut the braces and allowed the man-of-war to come up.

"Waal, I guess that saves yer bacon for ye," remarked the Sea Fox," but we'll see what the commodore has to say 'bout it when he comes aboard."

The vessels had drifted a few yards apart by now and the Sea Fox saw that some of his men were splicing the cut braces while others were washing the blood from the poop. Whereupon he sent the six white men who had been with him on the man-of-war back in the whaleboat with Robin Hood, giving orders to the latter to hoist up the boat and then have all the men line the rail of the *Wild Pigeon* as he wished to address them.

In a few minutes the slavers were at the rail and as their skipper crossed the quarter-deck of the *Bainbridge* to speak to them they cheered him vociferously.

"Thank ye, boys. Thank ye, hearty," he boomed. "I guess you're all right now, Tom Dollar'll be yer skipper home an' settle accounts with ye there, but I won't be long behind ye. That's 'nough said."

He glanced to leeward, where Gregory with his prize under all sail was in plain sight, not over two miles away, and reaching up to them with a stiff breeze.

"You'd better shake a leg an' be makin' the best o' yer way home, Tom Dollar," he advised, "if ye don't wanta be a-shakin' hands with the commodore. 'Twould be the end o' a puffeck day for him if he could capture ye now." Seeing the mouth of his mate fly open and anticipating the question Tom Dollar was about to ask, he added, "No, Tom Dollar, I can't go with ye, 'tain't possible. I promised Gregory I'd take charge o' his ship till he came back, an' I gotta do it. So pile the muslin on the old gal an' get outa here quick's ye can."

Knowing the futility of attempting to dissuade his skipper, Tom Dollar waved his hand in a farewell and began barking orders to his men.

"Give my regards to the fellers at the Astor House bar, Tom Dollar, but don't say nothin' 'bout me bein' the capt'in of a United States man-o'-war," the Sea Fox shouted, as the *Wild Pigeon's* sails filled and she began to draw away. "Not knowin' the innards o' the case they wouldn't b'lieve ye nohow."

THE RETURN OF THE SEA FOX

A $5,000 reward on his head the French thought would keep the Sea Fox clear of the slave markets of the West African coast—but to a Yankee skipper hot on the trail of vengeance of what importance are a few more scheming enemies?

"**W**AY 'NOUGH, men! In oars an' stand by to heave the painter to that pelican-faced Johnny Crappo a-leanin' over the rail thar."

The rays of the blazing African sun were lancing the glassy bosom of the Gulf of Guinea this July afternoon as the longboat pulled by five sweat-drenched seamen and steered by a short, thick-set man of about forty, with stringy brown hair falling over his ears, and a black silk patch covering his left eyelid, glided smartly up to the gangway of the French corvette, *L'hirondelle*.

With his hand on the Jacob's ladder the sturdy little officer spoke again, lowering his voice almost to a whisper.

"I'm takin' des'prit chances in boardin' this here man-o'-war, y'know, men; an' if so be that they clap me in irons get back to yer ship as soon's ye can. The mate 'ull know what to do in that case. So kinder stand by for squalls!"

He swarmed up the ladder and upon gaining the broad deck of the corvette cast a searching, apprehensive glance at the groups of white-uniformed men gazing at him listlessly from the shade formed by the great sails hanging windless against the spars. Observing that there was no sign of recognition on their bronzed faces, he drew a deep breath of relief and made his way to the quarter-deck with such an air of easy assurance that the prim master-at-arms hovering near made no attempt to inquire his business aboard.

Four hammocks containing fever-patients were strung from

the mizzen stay to the rigging, and the eyes of a fore-topman in
one of them happened to fall on the visitor as he waddled aft.
A puzzled expression came over the patient's drawn features
and he passed a wasted hand over his brow as if trying to recall
memories that had long lain dormant. And he kept his eyes fixed
on the short man until the latter disappeared under the awning.

"Arternoon, Capting!" greeted the newcomer cheerily in
Spanish—the language of the coast—to a slim, large-featured
man, sprawling in a deck-chair, his gold-buttoned uniform coat
flung open and a moist handkerchief in his hand.

Captain Seguenot arched his black eyebrows inquiringly and
indicated a chair nearby.

"Cap'n Ezra Hooter's my name, o' the Plymouth fam'ly o'
Hooters, y'know," the Yankee went on garrulously, pulling a
frayed, red, polka-dotted handkerchief and mopping his face
vigorously as he sank into the chair. "Jumpin' Judith!" he interjected. "If all hell's as hot as this I hope to marcy I don't anchor
thar. Waal, as I was a-sayin', I'm a Hooter an' that's my vessel
over yonder," he pointed to a brigantine with immensely long
yards and a terrific hoist to her mainsail, which had drifted into
sight of the corvette half an hour or so ago and was now swaying in the calm about three-quarters of a mile distant. "She's
the *Wind Flower* o' Noo York, trader, an' bound to Ole Calabar.
I knowed that nat'ally you'd wanta know what I was a-doin' in
these here waters so I brung my papers for ye to take a squint
at. Sorta killin' two birds with one stun', Capting, for I'm hopin'
to make some sorta deal with ye."

Captain Seguenot interchanged an amused smile with his
first lieutenant, who was leaning against the skylight, and fell
to work examining the sheaf of papers which Cap'n Hooter had
produced from an inside pocket.

"Your papers are quite in order, Captain Hooter," decided the
navy captain, handing them back to him. "But you could have
saved yourself the trouble of pulling all the way over in this heat.
Mon Dieu! I do believe my eyes are stewing in their sockets. I

was about to send Mr. Murat, the second lieutenant—"he waved a hand in the direction of the binnacle near which stood a well set young man with smiling dark eyes and pleasant features, examining the lense of a telescope—"over in the whaleboat to board you when you yourself lowered."

He was fanning himself with his handkerchief as he said this and so did not notice the strange gleam which came into the eyes of the Yankee upon learning the name of the second lieutenant.

Giving the latter a stabbing sort of stare Cap'n Hooter turned to the captain.

"Waal, as I was a-sayin'," he continued. "I come mostly to see if I couldn't make a deal with ye, Capting. I s'pose ye know the Sea Fox's busted outa that French prison he was a-doin' ten years in for slavin' an—"

"My dear sir," interrupted Captain Seguenot, with another smiling look at his first officer. "That news is stale. Very. I was on this ship here, lying in the harbor of Brest when he broke out of prison. It created quite a sensation, I remember, on account of the unique and daring manner in which the Sea Fox made his escape. One fine morning the guard coming to relieve the night sentry, whose duty it was to pace the yard beneath the prison cells, found him gagged and dangling high in the air by a rope the Sea Fox had made out of his blankets. The prisoner had managed somehow to saw through the bars on his window and, after lassoing the sentry and gagging him, had left him hanging to the lower ends of the bars. Nothing has been seen or heard of the Sea Fox since although there was some rumor of his having gone to Portugal. That was, let me see, about six months ago. It is doubtful, however, if the Sea Fox ever returns to this coast for the Governor of San Luis, the Senegal, has offered a reward of $5,000 for his capture. That will have a tendency to make it too warm for him around here, I believe."

Cap'n Hooter started to laugh, but checked himself.

" 'Twill take more'n that to stop the cuss, looks like," he remarked, then paused and added impressively, "for salt me down for a codfish, gentlemen, if he ain't right here this very minute in Old Calabar."

"What!" exploded Captain Seguenot, springing to his feet, his face betraying no little apprehension; "Captain Pepper here on the coast? In God's name, sir, how do you know this?"

CAP'N HOOTER adjusted the black patch over his eye and got to his feet, pointing a thick carroty finger at his beautiful craft.

"That hooker, gentlemen, used to be named the *Wild Pigeon* when the Sea Fox sailed her, an' there ain't a keel in any seas or in any weather can overhaul her," he declared. "An' I'm ordered to turn her over to Duke Ephraim, the King o' Calabar, y'know, who is acting for the Sea Fox. I've already got the passage money back to Ameriky for me an' my crew in my safe aboard her."

Captain Seguenot and the first lieutenant looked at each other for a moment; then the former turned suddenly to Captain Hooter, his eyes probing into the Yankee's.

"You must have some object in telling me this, Captain?" he questioned.

"To be sure I has an' no mistake, Capting," rejoined the little skipper, his one black eye gleaming with a sudden flare.

"Didn't I tell ye I had a deal on? In the fust place, howsumever, as a deacon o' the Chintonville Congrega'list church this ain't no fit job for me nohow. An' I wouldn't a-took it only I was outa a berth at the time this billet was offered me an' I got a wife an' six children a-lookin' to me for food an' clothes. I want to keep the *Wild Pigeon* for myself an' nat'ally ye wanta capter Cap'n Pepper."

At this juncture Louis Murat, the second lieutenant, happened to be passing, and, catching the name of the internationally known slaver, he turned his head with a jerk of surprise and stopped to listen. Cap'n Hooter flashed on him the look of a man who has found what he has been searching for and went on to say that he had been laying off and on the coast for the last three days waiting for some French cruiser to come along, as, according to French law, the informer was given the captured slave-vessel or its value in money; whereas with other nations the vessel was invariably destroyed, the informer merely getting a nominal reward.

"So ye see I had to come to you or some other cruiser o' yer nation," he finished.

Captain Seguenot's eyes showed a glint of contempt, for he now appraised the Yankee as one of those canting hypocrites who, under the cloak of religion, conceal their treachery and greed.

"You mean you will help me capture the Sea Fox if in return for your services I permit you to keep his vessel. Is that it, Captain Hooter?"

"Eggsactly! An' here's my plan. You put a dozen o' yer men in charge o' the second loo'ten't aboard my ship right now. I then take the ship into Ole Calabar an' turn her over to Duke Ephraim accordin' to my orders, d'ye see. Then arter the Sea Fox gets outside the Calabar bar with his cargo o' slaves yer men are to take her over an' capter the Sea Fox. Ye can be outside waitin' to give 'em a hand if nec'sary, but it won't be for I'll arrange with some o' my crew that I can trust to ship with the Sea Fox an' join forces with Mr. Murat. Then arter ye land yer slaves you turn the vessel over to me. Ye get the prize money for the slaves an' the honor o' recapterin' that ornery slaver an' I get a fine craft. How does that strike ye, Capting?"

The boyishly handsome face of Lieutenant Murat, who had been drinking in every word, flushed with a joyously eager expression.

"Just the thing!" he exclaimed impulsively. "Do let me go. Captain Seguenot!"

The latter smiled, scratched his chin thoughtfully, and shook his head.

"I can understand your anxiety to go, Mr. Murat," he observed, "but the Sea Fox is too clever to be caught in that manner. He'd smell a rat the moment he saw my men in uniform."

Cap'n Hooter surveyed him pityingly. "Jumpin' Judith, Capting!" he exclaimed. "I didn't figger that way 'tall. The men ain't to wear their uniform till they is ready to bust on deck an' take the ship over, d'ye see. You're to have the men fixed up in ole dungarees an' I'll interduce 'em aboard as distressed seamen what you took'n off'n the Salvages Islands. I'll explain that ye turned 'em over to me, seein' as how you're bound south o' the line an' the men wanta work their way on some coaster to French Assini."

"That sounds feasible. But how do you know positively that the Sea Fox is in Calabar?" persisted Captain Seguenot. In the service he was noted for being a very careful man.

For answer Cap'n Hooter stepped to the rail and called one of his men out of the boat. In another minute an alert, hawk-eyed, young New Yorker, about the same build as the second lieutenant, came running along the deck and saluted.

"Gallagher," commanded Cap'n Hooter, "tell the Capting here what he wants to know. Ye can speak unresarvedly!"

In answer to the naval man's questions as to what his ship was doing on the coast Gallagher's statement was practically the same as his skipper's.

"How did you first learn that the Sea Fox was in Calabar?" asked Captain Seguenot finally.

"Sure, an' it's no secret aroun' shippin' circles in New York, sir," replied Gallagher, grinning broadly. "Faith, an' the day we sailed wasn't they layin' bets up in the Astor House bar that the Sea

Fox would land a cargo of niggers in the States afore another five months was out."

CAPTAIN SEGUENOT frowned and his jaws set grimly.

"So that's the way of it, eh!" he grated. "We'll see about that." All doubts now swept aside, he turned to the second lieutenant, who was regarding him with an imploring look. "Pick your twelve men, Mr. Murat, get into dungarees all of you, and go with Captain Hooter. Our ships are to keep in sight of each other until we are off the Bakasi Banks, and when you arrive in Calabar, Captain, and see the Sea Fox send me word immediately by one of the kroomen."

Overjoyed the young lieutenant darted away, and in less than fifteen minutes he and a dozen brisk-looking sailors with their uniforms wrapped snugly under their arms were getting into the Yankee's boat.

As Cap'n Hooter came off the quarter a puff of wind shot down as the huge topsail slammed against the mainmast and lifted the hat and wig he was wearing so as to partly disclose his shining bald pate. The little skipper hastily pushed them back into place and was looking around to see if the incident had passed unobserved when, happening to glance at the hammock in which lay the fore-topman, he was not a little disturbed to see the sick man supporting himself on one elbow, his eyes starting from his head in a paroxysm of amazement. His mouth was writhing horribly as he strove to give expression to his thoughts, and, his fever-riven system suddenly giving way under the strain, he fell back in a dead faint.

Captain Seguenot and the others were so intent on the men's departure that this little by-play passed unnoticed, for which Cap'n Hooter felt mighty thankful.

"Holy mac'rel! But that was a close call!" he muttered cryptically and hurried down into the boat.

In fact he did not breathe with a full degree of easiness until his passengers and men were aboard the brigantine and, a light breeze having sprung up, she at once braced in her yards and headed away on her course.

The *L'hirondelle* had no sooner trimmed her sails and swung into the same course as the Yankee craft than the attention of the master-at-arms was attracted by the sight of the fore-topman sitting bolt upright in his hammock and staring about wildly. Upon catching sight of the vanishing brigantine he clutched spasmodically at his throat as if he were tearing the words from his lips.

"T-the Sea Fox—my God!" he screamed. "That was he— aboard here—on this very deck—"

"Seems Jean here is a little delirious with the fever, sir," the master-at-arms told the surgeon, who at that moment approached the hammock. "He's raving about that Yankee slaver, the Sea Fox. Probably because he was one of the crew of the frigate *Araignee* that captured the Sea Fox, you know, sir."

"No, I ain't off my head!" declared the sick man, with a determined air. "That was the Sea Fox what was aboard here just now. I've seen him too often aboard the *Araignee* to be mistaken."

"The Sea Fox that simple, farmer-looking person—impossible!" declared Captain Seguenot, thunderstruck, upon being told of Jean's revelation.

But after questioning the fore-topman there was no doubt left in his mind that Cap'n Hooter was indeed the great slaver. Moreover, he had had the staggering audacity to shanghai his second lieutenant and twelve of his finest men in broad daylight and before the eyes of the whole ship's company.

"He doubtless picked on us," gloomed the first lieutenant, "because we are newly arrived on the Coast and there was small chance of anybody aboard here having seen him before. But, even so, I can't fathom his motive in decoying our men."

"The reason he picked this ship, Mr. Berard," rejoined Captain Seguenot somberly, "was on account of Mr. Murat being aboard here. And the Sea Fox's motive is revenge: young Murat is a brother of the man who captured him—Commodore Murat of the frigate *Araignee*."

His troubled eyes swept across the wind-fretted sea to where the *Wild Pigeon*, with a fresh breeze on her quarter, was rushing headlong into a wall of purple mist. Another minute and she had vanished, engulfed in the vapor.

"That is the last we shall see of that intriguing devil," he burst out bitterly, "until he gets ready to strike!"

HELL TO pay and no pitch hot. Two days later Commodore Auguste Murat, coming up from the south on his frigate *Araignee*, fell in with the *L'hirondelle*, awaiting him off the mouth of the Calabar River. Naturally the first thing he heard was the news that the Sea Fox had swooped down and carried off his brother Louis and twelve French sailors.

The choleric commodore immediately went into a spasm of rage, during which he swore by all the gods of war that he would rest neither day nor night until he had laid that blankety blank Yankee slaver by the heels and had him put away for at least twenty years in the calabosa.

Accordingly he scoured the Calabar River with boats from both his ships in search of the elusive quarry for two days, only to learn through a Mpongwe spy—sent by the Sea Fox—that the slaver had not touched at Calabar at all but had proceeded eighty miles farther up the coast to Bonny. After digesting this information the commodore issued orders for the ships to crowd on all sail for the Bonny River.

He had hardly arrived off the bar, however, when Krinji, the chief spy of the native order of Egbo, of which the Sea Fox was the only white member, boarded him with a note which, stripped of a few errors in spelling and grammar, read:

> *Npane Creek, Bonny,*
> *Wed., July 21, 1847.*
> *Commodore Auguste Murat, Frigate* Araignee,
> *Commanding French Naval Forces, Coast of Africa.*
> *Sir:—Your brother, Louis Murat, and his twelve men are aboard*

my ship, the Wild Pigeon, *and in excellent health. If you wish them to return to you in that condition you will at once order your forces to refrain from any hostile act toward me until I am clear of the coast.*

May I state that I have a witch-doctor here who understands perfectly the art of using the bone-chisel and permanent dyes by which a no-account white man is occasionally reduced to a state of partial idiocy and transformed into a shining black slave for the Cuban plantations. Be wise in time. Rest satisfied with your commodore's epaulets and the red ribbon of the Legion of Honor bestowed on you by your Government for perjuriously sending an innocent foreigner to a French prison. Enough said.

Cap'n Barnabas N. Pepper.

Upon reading this the whites of the commodore's eyes became webbed with little red veins as his blood boiled with this added fuel to the flame. But just as he was about to explode he checked himself, his face going white at the thought of his brother, the only being on earth he really loved, in the power of the Sea Fox.

The letter sent the commodore in retrospection to the time when, twenty-one months ago, one morning he had boarded a French slaving-schooner about thirty miles to the westward of Sierra Leone. It was a shocking sight that met his eyes. Slaves and crew lay huddled about the deck, their eyes a huge mass of disease and all totally blind. A little scarecrow of a man with his left lower eyelid swollen to the size of a man's fist staggered along the deck and, muttering incoherently, fell senseless at the navy officer's feet. It was the Sea Fox, and for ten days and nights he had navigated the ship unaided. He was put aboard the frigate and later sent to the military hospital, where his left eye had to be removed.

Going into the cabin of the schooner Murat found in the captain's stateroom a man with heavy white bandages about his eyes. Immediately upon hearing a French naval officer addressing him he ripped off the bandages and disclosed two healthy, piercing black eyes. His name he said was Joseph Belanger and he was the captain of the schooner. He had taken the precaution of covering his eyes, he said, and kept below in order to avoid catching the disease with which the rest were infected. Then, to save himself from a long prison term, Belanger proposed to Murat that they destroy the ship's papers and let him come aboard the frigate as one of the crew; until the ship got in to port, when he would quietly disappear. By so doing it would be made to appear that the Sea Fox had been in command of the schooner and Murat would have the glory of capturing the great slaver. With visions of certain promotion before his eyes Murat had agreed readily to this proposition and it was carried out.

Barely able to leave the hospital, the Sea Fox—a pitiable figure with his wasted limbs and eyeless socket—was put on trial in St. Louis. He told his story with such an air of sincerity that, though all in the courtroom were familiar with tales of his artfulness, the majority of the spectators were convinced that he was telling the truth.

He stated that he was bound home with a cargo of slaves when one morning in Lat. 9—4N. Lon. 17—49W, he sighted a French schooner flying distress signals, boarding her he found that the slaves and crew were suffering from purulent opthalmia in its most virulent form. It had first appeared among the slaves, probably due to having been confined in the vitiated air between decks for over four days during a gale. It had then spread among the crew until, at the time he boarded her, all were blind except the mate. Her captain, Belanger, was blind in his stateroom, which he never left while the Sea Fox was aboard.

Seeing this terrible state of affairs, he had at once put his own ship, the *Wild Pigeon,* in charge of Tom Dollar, his mate, with orders to make the best of his way home, while he himself took command of the French schooner at her mate's request, as the latter knew nothing of navigation. The mate and five of the crew had died later on, just when he couldn't say exactly for he had been suffering pretty badly with the disease himself and things had got sort of hazy toward the last. But he had managed to keep the ship on her course to Freetown, the nearest port, until picked up by the *Araignee.*

Captain Murat then took the stand and swore that he had found no papers aboard the *Guepe* to prove that there ever had been any other captain aboard but the Sea Fox. He himself had found no captain or officers in the cabin when he had boarded her. He had been unable to get any statement from the few French sailors of the crew as they were blind and nearly insane with fever, but, knowing the astuteness of the prisoner, he was firmly convinced that the Sea Fox had attempted to leave the coast with two cargoes of slaves, one in the *Wild Pigeon* and the other in the schooner *Guepe*. He therefore urged that the prisoner be given a severe sentence as he had been engaged in the nefarious traffic for many years and his conviction would have a salutary effect on other slavers. The judge summed up the case in much the same spirit and imposed a sentence of ten years in the Brest prison.

The Sea Fox sat with bowed head as if stunned until aroused by the guard snapping the handcuffs on his wrists. A deep objecting murmur ran about the courtroom as the little slayer was led away.

"By Jove!" cried one ruddy-faced English naval officer, jumping up in his seat. "There's a sample of French justice for you. A poor Yankee risks his life and loses an eye trying to help some of their race and they put him in jail for ten years. Rotten, I call it! Bah!"

IT WAS plainly evident, mused the commodore, that the Sea Fox had known that the *Guepe* carried papers showing that Belanger was her captain, which, if produced at the trial, would have completely exonerated the Yankee slaver and proved that he was solely engaged in succoring a distressed people. As neither the captain or the papers appeared in court, the Sea Fox naturally deduced that the commodore had framed him in order to gain a much coveted promotion. Which, the commodore confessed to himself, was exactly the case.

In revenge, apparently, Cap'n Pepper had artfully spread his net and had already bagged the commodore's brother. Would he be the next, he wondered, or would the Sea Fox use the brother in some subtle manner as a means of driving home his reprisal? The commodore didn't know. Whether he liked it or not he was forced to wait for the slaver's next move. And it was this dubious waiting, this excoriating suspense, which now harassed him to an unbearable degree.

Feeling as if he were stifling, he went on deck and looked at the shore to where heavy, portentous clouds were sweeping-over the green Nahia hill and filling the mangrove-bordered gulf over the river with long streamers of vapor. Borne on the humid land-breeze, there drifted into his nostrils the fever-laden breath of Africa, a composite odor of monstrous, slime-dripping blooms, decaying vegetation, steaming mud-banks and putrid offal.

Depressed almost to the verge of nausea, he turned away and the next moment was handed a note by Smoke-jack, a krooman, who had just come aboard with it. Commodore Murat ripped open the cheap envelope and, as he read, his whole frame expanded with a mighty thrill of joy. His greatest enemy, the Sea Fox, was marked for destruction. The note ran:

Bonny, July 21, 1847.

Commodore Murat, Frigate Araignee.
Sir:

We, the undersigned, are prepared to deliver into your hands, without fail, the Yankee slaver Sea Fox, aboard of your ship on or about midnight tonight. In return for this service you must give a written agreement to the following terms:

1—After the Sea Fox has been turned over to you Captain Belanger is to be allowed to continue his voyage without having his vessel, the L'aigle, *searched. 2—You are to give Captain Belanger an order on the Governor of San Luis for $3,000 of the reward money and another order on the governor in favor of Jabez Codd, trader of Bonny, for the remaining $2,000, as that is the way we have mutually agreed to divide the reward. Please write your agreement on the back of this sheet and return by bearer.*

Signed: Captain Joseph Belanger,
Master of Brig L'aigle.
Jabez Codd, Trader of Bonny.

P.S. In case anything upsets our plans we will let you know, but at the present writing we are positive they will go through.

With the blood rioting joyously through his veins. Commodore Murat walked animatedly to the chart-room and wrote on the back of the letter: "I agree unreservedly to your terms," signed it and despatched it at once by Smoke-jack. Then he looked at his watch. Eleven o'clock. Long before that time next morning he would have the tables turned and the Sea Fox under hatches. The release of his brother and the men would follow, naturally.

What a wonderful coincidence, he thought, that Belanger should be in Bonny just at the opportune moment—not knowing of course that the Sea Fox had been nearly a month maneuvering to create that situation as well as the one in which he had gone off with the navy men. Nor would the commodore have felt so highly elated had he known that Smoke-jack, who ostensibly followed fishing for a livelihood, was an Egbo spy and that before the conspirators' letter had reached the commodore's hands it had been steamed open over a spirit-lamp by Cap'n Pepper and its contents read with much interest.

AFTER READING the letter Cap'n Pepper, highly tickled at the prospect of seeing his plans speedily brought to a successful issue, made a surreptitious trip ashore to look over the slaves in Captain Belanger's barracoons a quarter mile to the south of Bonny. He returned aboard the *Wild Pigeon* shortly before noon and, slumping into a chair under the poop-awning, mopped his stoical, crag-like brow vigorously.

"Waal, there'll be a showdown tonight an' I'm mighty glad on't!" he observed to Tom Dollar, the mate, a gaunt, whalebony individual with a face as long as a horse's. Stuffing into his port jaw a quid that raised a lump in his lean cheek the size of a gull's egg, the mate flirted a drop of sweat from the end of his hawk's-bill nose and fixed his gravel-gray eyes on the skipper inquiringly.

"One thing," continued the latter, "because I don't know the minute when that thar French lufftenant an' his men we got aboard here might l'arn somehow that Cap'n Hooter is the Sea Fox an' that I'm him, d'ye see. In course all our own men is keerful's can be, but it's a strain on all hands jes' the same." He pulled the patch over his left eye down a little and went on, half-musingly.

"A knowledge o' human nater is half the science o' war, Tom Dollar, an' once I know the character o' a man I know jes' what he'll do under sartain circumstances. I lets Belanger hunt me up instead o' me him—he thought so anyway—an' while he's explainin' that he was so blind an' ravin' with fever that he knowed nothin' about my bein' tried an' sent to the calabosa till two months arterwards. I could see that $5,000 reward money a-stickin' right outa his eyes. Blind, hell! Didn't I see him one day through the skylight o' the *Guepe* a-layin' in his bunk an' lookin' over the ship's papers? But as he would 'a' been wuss than useless on deck I never said nothin' an' at the trial I seen 'twas no use. They had me framed right an' no mistake. An' Belanger thinks he's got me now all slicked an' primed for a hog-killin'. An—hello!" he interrupted himself. "Here comes his pardner, Trader Codd, now."

He pointed to the mouth of the creek some distance away at a canoe containing a kroo paddler and a white man dressed in a linen suit.

"I invited him to eat here this noon for a special purpose," the Sea Fox chuckled. "I ain't got no grudge a'gin' him, as I knows on, for I'm as sartain as can be that Belanger talked him into helping trap me. But Codd nater'ally is mean 'nough to steal the acorns off'n a blind hawg so I don't feel no qualms in usin' him for my purpose, d'ye see, Tom Dollar."

The latter jerked the upper half of his lank body forward like a jack-knife and squirted a gill of tobacco juice over the rail.

"The hull cussed lot," he blazed, "commodore, Belanger, an' this here Codd, are nuthin' but the two ends an' the bight of a three-stranded cussed rogue!"

"Eggsactly," agreed the Sea Fox, and went off to find the lieutenant.

"Take a good look at this feller that's goin' to board us," Cap'n Pepper told him. " 'Tis the Sea Fox. Then keep outa sight, for he's mighty suspicious. That's why he came here to Bonny instead o' Calabar as we expected, y'know—"

Young Murat nodded and drew a deep breath at the prospect of seeing the great slaver of whom he had heard so many tales of daring.

"Here he comes, now!" added the skipper. "Jump afore he sees ye!"

Murat leaped behind the mainmast and, peeking around, saw a short, stout man, with bristling red mustaches, a purple, bulbous nose rooted between two watery blue eyes, coming over the rail. The navy officer felt a distinct twinge of disappointment, for this man hardly seemed capable of the swiftness, mobility, and penetration which he had heard attributed to the Sea Fox.

Unaware of the honor just conferred on him, the gin-reeking trader greeted the Yankee skipper heartily and they went below. After an hour trader Codd came on deck again, his nose a deeper shade of purple.

"Don't fail to be at Belanger's farewell party tonight as you promised, Captain," he reminded as he got into his canoe and shoved off.

"Never fear! I wouldn't miss that champagne," the Sea Fox called after him. Then with a peculiar smile still lingering about the corners of his mouth he joined Lieutenant Murat and told him that the Sea Fox had changed his plans. He had decided not to use the *Wild Pigeon* himself while there was a cruiser outside the bar. Instead he had arranged with a Captain Belanger for the use of his lighter-draft brig, the *L'aigle*. They intended to load her with slaves that night and go through the Kra Kramer Creek into the Sombrero River and to sea that way, thus avoiding the cruiser now hovering off the Bonny Bar.

Then the *Wild Pigeon* was to get under weigh the next morning, and as there was nothing incriminating aboard her she could pass the cruiser. The two slave ships were to meet at Princes Island, 160 miles to the southward, when the slaves would be transhipped to the *Wild Pigeon.*

At this information the frank countenance of the young navy officer shaded into a look of bitter disappointment as he saw his chance of capturing the great Sea Fox go glimmering. The Yankee skipper laid a hand on his shoulder.

"Don't heave-to in the doldrums yet, Lufftenant," he encouraged. "Listen keerful now."

He looked around to see there was no one within hearing and then talked stirringly for the next eight minutes, at the duration of which Lieutenant Murat, glowing with delight, grasped his hand and shook it heartily.

"It will be gorgeously exciting!" exclaimed the volatile Frenchman.

" 'Twill, an' then some," agreed the Sea Fox, grimly.

NIGHT FELL and the stars came bubbling out. Captain Belanger, saturnine, yellow as a lemon, the wings of his long nostrils continually drawn upward as if they smelled something disagreeable, gave a nervous pull to his pointed mustaches and shook hands with Cap'n Pepper, who, that moment, came over the rail of the *L'aigle.* Trader Codd, who had been aboard for some time, also clasped the Yankee's hand, shaking it with the warmth of an old-time friend.

"Ah, it is very kind and gracious of you to come and see me before I set off on my venture," spouted the French skipper in honeyed accents as he led the way below to where a supper, smoking savorily in dishes on the table, awaited them.

After the meal they sat on the poop, smoking and chatting until, as the great African moon shot above the palms back of the squat town of Bonny, Captain Belanger glanced nervously at his watch.

"I hope that damnable *nafouca* (slave-broker) gets my niggers started in time," he grated. He glanced slyly at the Sea Fox.

"I want to take advantage of the tide when it begins to set through Kra Kramer Creek. I'll have to go out that way, you know, Captain, in order to avoid that meddling cruiser. Ah, here comes the first twenty of my niggers now," he added as a canoe full of blacks appeared in the glittering wake of the moon and paddled up to the gangway.

Belanger and his guests walked to the break of the poop and watched the slaves as they were checked off by the mate and a man holding a lantern. When they had disappeared down the hatchway the Sea Fox yawned, and after thanking Belanger for his hospitality and wishing him a quick passage, declared that it was time for him to go aboard his own ship. The French skipper laid a protesting hand on his arm.

"Just remain a few minutes longer, Captain, and you can go," he urged. "I have a little present I wish to give you as an expression of my regret over that deplorable state of affairs which made it impossible for me to testify in your behalf at the trial. Come below and I will give it to you, and at the same time we'll all have a parting glass."

The Sea Fox divined that the crucial moment had arrived. He held his watch up to the moonlight—10:33 o'clock. Then he looked in the direction of his vessel, but though she was anchored but a little distance from the *L'aigle* she was completely hidden in the deep shadow of the wooded creek-bank. But on the edge of this shadow the Sea Fox fancied that he could make out something moving, something like the shape of a canoe creeping toward the brig.

"Jumpin' Judith!" he mentally ejaculated. "Things 'ull begin to hum soon or I'm a Dutchman." This was true in more ways than one, for the Sea Fox had no sooner followed his host and Trader Codd into the after cabin, which was softly illumined by a hanging lamp, when Belanger, swift as light, clapped a pistol to his head.

"Wh—what's the meanin' o' this, I'd like to know?" quavered

the Sea Fox, pretending to be greatly agitated. "A helluva way to treat a invited guest, I must say!"

Captain Belanger, grinning like a hyena, stepped back a foot or two, still keeping his pistol leveled.

"Ah, my dear sir!" he gloated. "I wished to show you that the French eagle is swifter than the American fox. You are going back to your den in the Brest prison, sir. It is really funny, Captain!"

"Waal, prob'ly 'tis sorta funny, lookin' at it your way," admitted the Sea Fox, sparring for time. "I s'pose Commodore Murat 'ull let ye run a cargo o' slaves by him now as well as givin' ye two the reward, eh?"

The French skipper's stinging rejoinder was frozen on his lips, for at that moment the quiet of night was split by the fierce hurrah of a boarding party followed by the swift stamp of hurrying feet along the decks.

"Now that's what I call navigatin', folks," chuckled the Sea Fox. "Seems like I had it timed to a minute, don't it?"

Belanger flung him a diabolical look and with a furious oath made a rush for the companionway. He was half-way up the steps when the doors were slammed violently in his face and a deep, menacing voice, which Cap'n Pepper recognized as belonging to his giant black bo'sun, Robin Hood, ordered him back into the cabin.

The Sea Fox greeted his return with a broad smile.

" 'Tain't so funny when it happens to ye, is it?" His hand dropped carelessly onto a heavy cut-glass decanter of brandy on the table at his side. "Looks like the fox had sorta played hell with the eagle's tail-feathers," he added. "You'll have a chance now to try some o' that prison stuff yerself, I guess."

MURDER, STARK and staring, leaped into the eyes of the maddened Frenchman. He was in the act of raising his pistol when the decanter, propelled by Cap'n Pepper's sturdy right arm, struck him squarely between the eyes and he crumpled senseless to the floor.

At the same time the doors to the companionway were thrown open and down into the cabin rushed Lieutenant Murat in full uniform, followed by Robin Hood and four of the boarders.

"Hurrah!" cried the navy officer, flouring his cutlass above his bare head, his eyes sparkling joyously. "Hurrah, Captain Hooter, it turned out just as you predicted. We took the ship without striking a blow. As soon as the crew saw us in uniform they all dove below and we put the hatches on. All I lost was my cap and that got knocked off somehow in the shuffle. Now you, Captain Pepper," he turned to the trader, who all this time had stood rooted to the spot going from one paroxysm of astonishment into another, "you are my prisoner. I shall have to lock you up and place you under guard."

"Gosh almighty!" shrieked the trader in dismay. "I ain't the Sea Fox. There he is—"

The rest of the sentence died in his throat as the great hand of Robin Hood closed on his windpipe. The Sea Fox quietly opened the door of an adjacent stateroom and the giant bosun, picking up the squirming trader bodily, threw him inside and, locking the door, handed the key to Lieutenant Murat.

"I had to knock this cuss out," explained Cap'n Pepper, pointing to the huddled form of the Frenchman on the floor. "He was a-goin' to shoot me. He's the skipper o' this brig an' pardner in this deal with the Sea Fox, d'ye see."

"Which means that he'll serve a long prison term as well. We've caught them both with the goods aboard." He then directed his men to lay him in the bunk in the next stateroom. When this was done and a sentry posted between the doors Murat turned to Cap'n Pepper. "By rights. Captain, you are entitled to part of the reward for it was entirely through your plans that the Sea Fox was captured, you know."

The Yankee slaver smiled and shook his head, saying that the *Wild Pigeon* was sufficient reward for what little he had done.

Meanwhile on deck Gallagher and five of his shipmates, who

had come with Robin Hood to aid Murat and his men, were going about quietly, cutting all the sheets, halliards, braces and other running gear, thus carrying out the previous orders of the Sea Fox, who wished to delay the brig until the *Wild Pigeon* had passed the bar.

In a few minutes the Sea Fox wished the lieutenant good luck with his prisoners, shook him heartily by the hand, and then took his men aboard the *Wild Pigeon*. The lieutenant then became so busily engaged in repairing his cut rigging, which he attributed to the malice of some of the seamen prisoners, and the shadows lay so densely about the Sea Fox's vessel, he was quite unaware that there was a steady stream of canoes loaded with Belanger's slaves leaving the shore and being diverted to the *Wild Pigeon* by Tom Dollar in a boat containing ten hard-bitted sailors armed with cutlass and pistol.

In less than an hour 570 A-No. 1 slaves were in the roomy hold of the Yankee brigantine and her boat hoisted on its davits.

"Hell's lifts! But I jest can't figger how the Cappen's a-goin' to git clear now," observed Tom Dollar to Robin Hood as they were getting the ship ready for sea. "I had an idee that the Cappen would keep them Johnny Crappos aboard here as a sorta secur'ty for our safety 'till we got to sea when we could let 'em have a boat to git back to the cruiser with. But blast me ef we've got anythin' now to fall back on. That commodore 'ull board us quick'n scat, I reckon."

SHORTLY AFTER midnight a rocket shot up from Field Point, where Commodore Murat had a lookout stationed.

"Look!" exclaimed the commodore, tensely, to his officers, all of whom had remained on deck in anticipation of catching the great slaver. "Belanger is coming out! There! See!"

The sky-scraping trucks and towering royal of a vessel could be seen rounding the point and the next minute she shot into view, her great sails stretching far out on either side of her long, black hull and gleaming like one bank of snow piled on top of another in the brilliant moonlight, the sea piling in a mass of flashing foam about her knife-like bows as she dashed into the long, heavy swells on the bar. Up went her tapering jib-boom, like an accusing finger pointed at the cruiser; a crash like a volley of musketry as her heavy canvass slapped against the spars; a long slide down the slope of the outer seas, and the beautiful craft was over the bar and heading directly for the frigate.

At this juncture one of the officers, who had been watching the oncoming vessel narrowly, ventured to observe that he had heard that Belanger was master of a full-rigged brig whereas this craft was unmistakably a brigantine.

"Well, that is an hermaphrodite brig, isn't it?" snapped the commodore. "This must be Belanger for if his plans had miscarried he would have let us known. And there is the proof," he added as he leveled his glasses on her, "he's got the French flag flying from his main truck so that we can see it easily and recognize him." He gave a gleeful chuckle. "Now we will soon have the Sea Fox in charge again. He didn't last long for all his reputed craftiness."

He then gave orders for the courses to be hauled up and the ship brought to the wind.

Meanwhile nearer and still nearer came the brigantine, swooping down on the frigate like some monstrous bird until all her rigging and running gear could be plainly discerned. Then of a sudden could be heard a voice aboard her, calm and distinct, giving an order in an unmistakable Yankee drawl that smote the commodore's ears and sent an icy shiver down his spine.

"Starb'd fore braces thar! Four p'ints, Mr. Dollar!"

Her yards were braced in a twinkling and the brigantine at once kept off to pass clear of the frigate's stern. This maneuver disclosed her entire port side to the view of all on the cruiser, and the crew from the commodore down were so thunderstruck at what they saw that they never noticed that the French flag was being hauled down and the Stars and Stripes sent fluttering to her peak. For their eyes were popping at the sight of a chain cable leading from the port anchor of the brigantine and stopped to the sheerpoles of the fore and main rigging. Seated on the rail amidships, with their backs toward the frigate and their hands lashed to the cable above their heads, was a man in the gold-laced cap and uniform of a French lieutenant and twelve men in navy whites.

A huge Negro, bare to the waist, the melting moonlight burnishing his great torso into gleaming bronze, stood by the cat-head with a top-maul in his hand ready to knock out the pin holding the ring-stopper and let the anchor go at the word of command.

"Louis—my brother!" moaned the commodore, his face the color of ashes. "My God, is that Sea Fox man or devil?"

His straining eyes saw a short, thick-set man spring into the port main rigging of the slaver and place his cupped hands to his lips. Then came the hail.

"Ahoy, the frigate. Commodore Murat, I'm in a hurry to get home. One horstile movement outa you an' I'll let that anchor go an' send your brother an' his men right kerplumux to hell thirty-two fathoms down. Hold yer hosses till I get outa range o' yer guns an' I'll turn yer men loose an' furnish 'em a boat to get back to the frigate. Good night, an' be damned to ye!"

This brought the commodore to life. With the veins standing out rigidly on Iris forehead and his features convulsed with impotent rage, the commodore dashed his glasses to the deck and, digging his fingernails into the quarter-rail, glared with flaming, bloodshot eyes at the stocky, imperturbable figure outlined so distinctly in the rigging.

"Keep her off three p'ints!" ordered the Sea Fox to the helmsman, leaping lightly to the deck as the *Wild Pigeon* flashed by the frigate's stern within half pistol shot. "Now, Tom Dollar, square yer yards, then set yer wind-drinkers an' let the ole gal go home. We fair had that commodore bluffed to a stan'still. Cussed if we didn't. 'Twas his guilty conscience what feazed him, Tom Dollar."

The Sea Fox himself slacked off the sheet of the great mainsail, thus completely concealing her decks from the view of the frigate. Then with roars of laughter some of the slavers jumped to the chain cable and, cutting the lashings, released their thirteen shipmates who had been impersonating the navy men.

"Jumpin' Judith, Gallagher," chuckled Cap'n Pepper, "but ye made a right smart lufftenant, an' that's a fac'. Good thing them nigger chiefs on the coast are so fond o' navy duds or I might not a-had the uniforms in my tradin' stock. As it was, Gallagher, ye had to steal Murat's cap to complete yer outfit."

HE TURNED and, walking aft, went up on the poop where in a few minutes he was joined by Tom Dollar, wearing a smile that split his face from ear to ear.

"I see you've shaken out a couple o' reefs in that long face o' yourn, Tom Dollar," remarked the Sea Fox. "What air ye a-grinnin' about, I'd like to know."

"Haw—haw—haw!" spluttered the mate, slapping his bony knees.

"May I swaller a nor'west gale if this ain't a leetle the best I ever did see in all my born days. Jest 'magine, Cappen, how many fits that thar commodore 'ull throw when his brother sails out in a coupla hours an' hands Codd over to him as the Sea Fox. 'Twould be as good's a circus to see it, Cappen."

The crag-like features of the Sea Fox kindled.

"Waal, that's a picter I've had in my mind all along, Tom Dollar. I has allus contended, ye know, that a moral revenge cuts deeper an' lasts longer'n a phys'cal one. An' we've paid off our scores an' here we be bound home with $150,000 worth o' slaves an' all clear velvet. That 'ull sorta recompense me for the fifteen months I spent eatin' sour black bread an' a-fightin' saber-toothed fleas in a Brest prison."

He paused and looked across the moonlit sea to where the frigate was rising and falling on the long swells, her sails still aback. Then he turned to Tom Dollar.

"But dang it all, somehow I allus feel kinda sorry for a man I get up into a corner, jes' the same," he added soberly.

THE SEA FOX CLAWS
TO WINDWARD

"The best laid plans of mice and men—" Jake Spiddy had his plans all laid; the Sea Fox had arranged his—and a pistol in the hands of a drunkard was to scramble them irreparably

"**T**HAT'LL DO! I'll swim the rest of the way, Twigg," said the big, sway-backed man, casting his shifty, pale-blue eyes onto the little, gnarled-featured man pulling the dinghy, as he stood up in the stern sheets.

"Lessee, it must be nigh about nine o'clock now," he grunted; "just the right time to pull this thing off." He gazed speculatively over the broad inky bosom of the Calabar River, spangled by the reflections of the blazing West African stars, to where, her long tapering spars etched sharply against the glare of the big evening bonfire in Duketown Square, lay the American slaver-brigantine, the *Wild Pigeon;* Cap'n Barnabas N. Pepper—the Sea Fox—master.

"What dev'ltry ye figgerin' on now, Jake Spiddy?" grumbled his elder brother, resting on his oars. "Why don't ye let me set ye alongside the *Wild Pigeon* with the boat?"

"An' have every cussed one of the crew see me boardin' her, eh!" flashed Jake Spiddy. "I thought ye knew what I was cal'latin' on. Didn't I tell ye I had to get the money from somewhere to pay for my cargo of slaves. We can't pay for 'em with a bundle of rope-yarns, can we? Waal, it's common knowledge that the Sea Fox allus carries a big pile of gold in his money chest, an' that's what I'm a-goin' for. I aim to sneak aboard his ship while the ship's company is busy yarnin' an' afore the anchor-watch is set for the night. Then I'll stow myself away in the lazareete somewhere an', when the Sea Fox goes ashore in the mornin' an' the rest of the crew are busy about the decks, I'll bust his money box an' help myself, see?"

"It's mighty resky, Jake!" squeaked the little mate. "I'd as soon go right inter hell's own hole as try it. Besides, how in tunket be ye goin' to get away with the money in broad daylight, I'd like to know?"

"Me an' Trader Graggs has arranged all that. There'll be a canoe handy for me to drop into when the coast is clear."

Jake Spiddy took up a hole in his belt and shifted the sheath holding a wicked, double-edged knife farther back so that it would not impede his thigh muscles. He was about to get into the water when Twigg Spiddy touched his leg where the trouser was rolled above the knee.

"Better not try it, Jake," he whined. "I feel plain's can be sunthin'll happen to ye. That there Sea Fox is too big a mack'rel for ye to handle, to my notion."

Jake Spiddy spat disgustedly into the river. "Damned if you've got the guts of a cockroach when the rum an' laud'num is out of ye, Twigg Spiddy. Who the hell's the Sea Fox anyway. Nothin' more'n a man. He'll be hollerin' for ice as loud's I be in the next world 'tis likely."

"Mebbe. But you'll be hollerin' fust, if ye ain't keerful," warned his brother.

The latter, with a scornful snort, eased himself into the water.

"Go back to our ship an' don't worry none about me," he said, with a hand on the gunwale. "It might hearten ye a little to know I've got another trick up my sleeve if this one fails. The Sea Fox can claw to wind'ard (maneuvering to get the weather-gauge of an enemy) till the devil's tail freezes, but I'll make him pay for my cargo of slaves somehow."

Letting go of the boat, he began to swim noiselessly with long, powerful strokes in the direction of the *Wild Pigeon* about two cable lengths (1,200 feet) away.

When within twenty feet or so of the slaver, which balked hugely above him in the starlight, Jake Spiddy stopped and began treading water while he carefully reconnoitered. He could hear the hum of voices on the fo'cas'le head where the sailors were yarning, and from the shore came the deep boom of the tomtoms borne on the gentle breeze which also carried to his nostrils the distinctive orchid-crushed-in-dung-smell of West Africa.

Having satisfied himself that everything so far favored the success of his plan, Jake Spiddy made his way cautiously toward the vessel. He arrived within a few feet of her hull when suddenly he came in contact with a half-grown specimen of that terror to the African natives, the *gymnotus electricus* or electric eel. The shock from a full grown one will easily overthrow a horse and this young one was quite capable of discharging enough voltage as it passed by to make Jake Spiddy imagine that something had torn his backbone out by the roots.

The unexpected encounter with this slimy monster threw him into a spasm of fear which, combined with the excruciating pain, forced a stifled groan from his white lips. Until the momentary paralysis had left his right leg and side he was obliged to flounder about in a half-circle to keep from sinking. He made but little noise, yet slight as it was it caught the quick ear of Tom Dollar, the lank, doughty mate of the *Wild Pigeon,* who at that moment had left his seat on the main hatch, where he had been chatting with Robin Hood, the giant Negro bosun, to squirt a gill or so of tobacco-juice over the rail.

"LISTEN, ROBIN HOOD!" intoned the mate "Damn'f there ain't sunthin' funny goin' on in the water."

The bosun sprang to his side, and they both caught sight simultaneously of the struggling Jake Spiddy.

"Hell's lifts!" roared the mate, lifting the whole right side of his lean face in a prodigious wink at the bosun. "If there ain't an ungodly kerlummux o' a big fish right alon'side our scuppers. Hand me the grains, quick, one o' ye!" this last to the sailors, who had come pouring off the fo'cas'le-head upon hearing the mate shout.

The grains, a four-pronged barbed instrument attached to a fourteen-foot pole, was immediately shoved into his hands, and, leaning far over the rail, the mate allowed it to drop onto the bulging and tightly drawn seat of Jake Spiddy's trousers. Instantly there was a great floundering in the water and the quiet night all became sulphurated with a lurid burst of profanity.

"Got him, by tophet if I hain't!" yelled the delighted mate. "Give a hand here to help haul him up, Robin Hood!"

The grinning bosun put two mighty hands on the pole and they hauled up on the wriggling prize, which was spitting like a wildcat in a trap. When nearly to the level of the rail the grains pulled out of the stout duck and Jake Spiddy soused back into the river, his last oath ending it a sputter.

One of the crew then got a running bowline about him with a "Yo-ho-ho-o-hh" the sailors walked away with the line, and the buccaroo, foaming with rage at being treated in this unseemly manner, came flying over the rail and hit the deck with a thump. Someone whisked the bowline from his legs and, a little dazed, he sprawled about the deck for a moment like a freshly caught lobster.

After a little he staggered to his feet—a dripping figure clad in a red flannel undershirt and soiled duck trousers—and peered about in the starlight at the grinning slavers.

"Sweet Jeeroos-a-lam!" he spat out. "If this don't beat hell a-yawnin'! Has I fell plumb into a blasted buzzard's nest, or what, I wanta know?"

The sailors rocked with laughter, at which Jake Spiddy's bold, hard features became black as a thunder-cloud. He did not relish being made a butt for this fo'cas'le scum, as he mentally termed them. Then he caught sight of Tom Dollar still holding the grains.

"So 'twas you, you sturgeon-backed sarpint ye, that harpooned me was it?" he bristled. "What d'ye mean by it? Lemme tell you that Cap'n Jake Spiddy is jest a mossel of the best man that ever cast a shadder on a ship's deck an' a bad man to fool with. Stand by now, for I'm a-comin'!"

Flying went the top button of his shirt as he violently tore open the collar and had set himself for a spring at the mate. But of a sudden a hush fell among the slavers.

"What's goin' on here?" a deep, authoritative voice almost at Jake Spiddy's elbow asked quietly.

Jake Spiddy spun half-way round and confronted a short, thick-set man whose cool, clean linen suit set off a figure as tough and square as a white oak bitt. Over his eyeless left socket he wore a green silk patch, which at that moment he adjusted with one freckled hairy hand with the other he waved at the sailors to disperse. They at once assumed a deferential air and went in a body to their quarters.

"I sorta guess you're the Sea Fox, or perhaps I should say Cap'n Pepper," inferred Jake Spiddy, affecting a cordial manner and extending his hand. "I'm Cap'n Jake Spiddy of the brig *Horatio*."

"What's this man doin' aboard my vessel, Mr. Dollar?" inquired the Sea Fox, ignoring the intruder altogether.

The mate replied that it was a mystery to him. He had first seen the stranger in the water alongside the ship and, thinking it was some rascally native intent on slipping aboard to steal something, he had given him a touch of the grains.

Feeling the penetrating black eye of the noted slaver boring into him, Jake Spiddy hastened to explain his presence there. He had pressing business, he said, with the Sea Fox. Had waited for some hours aboard his ship for the mate to return from shore with the dinghy and finally had been compelled to take a canoe. It had capsized in mid-stream and he was forced to swim the rest of the way to the ship.

"An' one of them blasted 'lectric eels threw a ten-ton charge into me an' put me plumb outa gear for a spell," he added. "An' on top of that I gets the grains square in my latter aind. Nacherally I was a little riled to be treated that fashion, specially as I was on an errand of mercy, ye might say."

The grimly powerful features of the Sea Fox relaxed into a smile.

"Pressin' business—errand o' marcy, eh," he ruminated, scratching the side of his short, freckled nose. "Good 'nough, Cap'n Spiddy; jes' come with me an' I'll be glad to listen to ye."

"I lost on the first deal but I'll hold all the cards on the next one," Jake Spiddy told himself as he followed Cap'n Pepper below to the cabin.

Here the latter seated his visitor in a chair under the rays of the hanging lamp while he himself chose a seat in the shadow.

Jake Spiddy squirmed a little at first under that probing searchlight of an eye which seemed capable of piercing every veil which falsehood draws before truth; he tried to shift his chair but discovered that it was screwed to the floor. However, his iron nerves combined with a brass-bound assurance soon put Jake Spiddy at his ease and he launched into the business at hand—to buck for the second time this fox, who, Jake Spiddy admitted to himself, looked in reality more like a stunted tiger.

"I COME over to tell you, Cap'n Pepper," began Jake Spiddy, "that there's a pore young countrywoman of ourn a prisoner on the *Break of Dawn,* that tradin' hulk layin' over there south of the town, y'know."

"Ole Bildad Graggs's hulk," interjected the Sea Fox, becoming interested. "Go on. What about this here female?"

"Did ye ever hear tell of a gal named Ruth Delway, Cap'n?" asked Jake Spiddy, bringing his shifty eyes to bear on the other.

"Why, yaas," rejoined the Sea Fox reflectively. "That was the name o' the gal that disappeared so myster'ous like from the brig *Abbie Dabbs* right here in this river more'n a year ago. I remember readin' about it in the shipping news. Why?"

"Why? 'Cause, Cap'n Pepper, Ruth Delway an' the gal on the hulk is one an' identickle."

"The hell ye say!" marveled the Sea Fox, jerking forward in his chair. "How d'ye know that, tell me?"

Jake Spiddy then related how he had been passing the hulk in his boat that afternoon when the girl had beckoned to him from a porthole. He had immediately pulled over to her and she had told him her story. She said that until a month ago she had been unable to recall her name or where she came from. Graggs had told her that he had found her living with some native women on the bank of Wiwa Creek. They claimed to have fished her out of the water. Then she had had a fever and her memory had been restored. Her name was Ruth Delway, she said, daughter of Captain Jules Delway, a West Coast trader on the brig *Abbie Dabbs*. She remembered that she had been ill with a fever aboard the brig, and probably in a delirious moment she must have jumped overboard and drifted into the creek where the native women found her.

"There ain't a doubt it's her all right, Cap'n," concluded Jake Spiddy. "She talked as straight's a gun-bar'l. Now she wants to get back home the wuss way, she says."

"H-mm! Myster'ous are the ways o' Providence!" mused the Sea Fox ironically. "This gal in a crazy fit jumps or falls overboard an' floats six miles up to the mouth of Wiwa Creek right inter the hands o' the natives. An', though her father has nearly all the kroomen on the Calabar huntin' for her, thar' she was right in plain sight, ye might say." He looked sharply at Jake Spiddy, who squirmed a little. "There's $5000 reward out right now for her or her body," added the Sea Fox. "I should think that weasel o' a Graggs 'ud been a-goin' arter it afore now!"

"That part's easy explained," rejoined Jake Spiddy. "The gal told me that Gragg's got so fond of her—treats her just like a darter, he does—that he won't let her go. Pretends that she's still outa her head, y'know. An' when he leaves the hulk he locks her in a stateroom. That's how she happened to see me this afternoon. That gal's Ruth Delway all right. There ain't a doubt of it in my mind."

The Sea Fox twirled his inevitable quill toothpick and looked at a brilliant-winged moth circling about the globe of the lamp.

"Waal," he averred finally. "Looks like you'd have to help the gal get back to her folks. A kind deed an' well paid for too, figgerin' in that reward, Cap'n Spiddy."

"Blow my shirt, that's just what I cal'lated on doin', Cap'n Pepper. I run my slaves to Cuby, y'see. I offered to take her aboard and send her home from Havana, but she thinks it would be best if she could go home direct with you."

"Me!" exclaimed the Sea Fox, his eye coldly suspicious. "What on airth does the gal know 'bout me, I'd like to gather?"

"Graggs told her, prob'ly. Anyway the pore gal begged me with tears in her eyes to see you as quick's I could and ask you to come over an' see her about two-thirty tomorrow afternoon. Her cabin porthole is the second abaft the mizzen riggin', starboard side."

Jake Spiddy got up as if to take his leave. The Sea Fox also rose and stood with one hand on the table pondering over the matter for some moments.

"Good 'nough!" he decided. "I'm mighty busy jes' now gettin' my niggers, d'ye see. Only got a hundred so far an' I need five hundred an' fifty to make a cargo; but I'll go over tomorrer an' see how the thing stan's."

He took a decanter of rum and a glass from the rack and poured out a stiff drink.

"Have a partin' glass, Cap'n Spiddy," he proposed, "an' then I'll have one o' my men set ye aboard yer ship."

Jake Spiddy drank the prime Old Medford and smacked his lips.

"The more I think about that pore lone gal aboard the hulk a-eatin' her heart out with homesickness the wuss I feel, Cap'n Pepper," he sighed, and, setting the glass down, he rolled his shifty eyes sorrowfully toward the deck-beams. "Seems like I oughta do my share in helpin' her, durned if it don't." Then, turning eagerly to the Sea Fox as if struck with a sudden thought, he burst out, "Sweet Jeeroos-a-lam, Cap'n Pepper, I can do sunthin' too. I've got four hundred and seven slaves ashore in Mongo Sanchez's barracoons, an' if you decide to give the gal a passage home I'll let you have them slaves of mine so's you can sail right away. Jest pay me what I paid for them, twenty-five dollar a piece, an' they're yours under them conditions."

The single eye of the Sea Fox glittered joyfully, for this was indeed a gilt-edged offer. It would take him at least three weeks longer before he could hope to get that number of slaves together.

"That sounds as good's Gunter to me, Cap'n," he approved.

"Just a minnit," went on Jake Spiddy. "By lettin' you have my slaves so's you can do an act of mercy it means I got to stay here nigh a month longer than I cal'lated on. That there means a lot of expense to me. Now I figger if I could get that reward that's offered for the gal I could come clear, y'see."

"Meanin' that ye think I oughta advance ye the reward, I s'pose," inferred the Sea Fox, scratching his massive chin thoughtfully. As a matter of fact he would gladly have given a bonus of five thousand dollars in any case.

"Eggzac'ly." The other skipper nodded. "The gal's folks will pay it back to ye when they get the gal, y'see."

"I'll tell ye what I'll do, Cap'n Spiddy," the Sea Fox announced after a moment's thought. "Arter Graggs goes ashore tomor-row arternoon I'll go over an' see the gal, an' if everythin' looks shipshape an' aboveboard I'll agree to yer terms an' thank ye for the chance.'Nough said. Now come on deck an' I'll have ye put aboard yer ship."

"H O W ' D   Y E   make out?" squeaked Twiggs a few minutes after his brother had returned to his ship.

"Good!" rejoined Jake Spiddy. "I'm a-ridin' a high tide." And he related what had happened.

Twigg shook his head ominously.

"I'm afeard o' that Sea Fox!" he quavered. "No one ever claws to wind'ard o' him on a deal, they say."

"Waal, little brother, Jake Spiddy has just done it. Haw-haw! He's goin' to pay me for slaves I ain't paid for myself yet, an' he's also goin' to give me five thousand dollars for a gal that—"

"S-hh! Don't talk so loud, Jake," expostulated the timid mate, peering about the gloomy quarter-deck. "Ye can't tell who's about."

Feeling the need of his accustomed stimulant, Twigg hurried below to his room, lighted the gimbal lamp, and took out of a locker a quart bottle of rum tinctured with opium. He poured a ship's tumbler two-thirds full of this mixture and gulped it down, his small, restless eyes quickly emitting a lurid glare as the potent liquor burned through his veins. Replacing the bottle, he leaned against his bunk and gradually felt stealing over him a reckless disregard for the Sea Fox or anyone else. Poor Twigg was now having his moment of glory. Almost constantly in a state of fear, under the influence of his doctored grog he went to the other extreme and for a pitifully short time revelled in the belief that he was qualified to become a bolder pirate than either Morgan or Teach. Accordingly his narrow shoulders straightened, the ragged nostrils of his thin, pointed nose quivered, and, opening his desk, he took out a heavy pistol. Shoving it into his pocket with a stick-at-nothing-air, he raced up onto the poop where, with eyes glaring and fingers working like a cat flexing its claws, he strode up and down.

"I can defy the hull, blasted world!" he muttered. "That's

Twigg Spiddy for ye. Bold's a lion; yes, by godfrey, two lions. Dam'f I ain't!"

Twigg's flaming glance swept over the bands of luminous ripples in the river to the *Wild Pigeon*, over whose fore yard the moon was just rising.

"The Sea Fox's vessel, is it?" he snarled drunkenly. "T'hell with him. Paugh! I'd fix him just like that!"

Jerking the pistol from his pocket, he discharged it in the direction of the *Wild Pigeon*.

Jake Spiddy, turning into his bunk, heard the report and smiled sardonically.

"Twigg's full of Dutch courage ag'in," he muttered, "an' is firin' blank charges as usual. Waal, there's no harm in the poor cuss; just sorta throwin' off his bile, I guess."

He rolled into his bunk under no apprehension, never suspecting that possibly in an insane moment Twigg might ram a bullet down on top of the charge of powder with dire consequences.

WATCHING THROUGH his glasses the following afternoon, the Sea Fox discerned the bowed form of old Bildad Graggs going ashore about two o'clock. This he did daily, returning about four. In another ten minutes the Sea Fox, hidden from the sight of anyone on shore by the thick growth of mangroves on the eastern bank, slipped the end of the dinghy's painter through one of the mizzen chainplates and allowed the boat to float back under the porthole of the stateroom in which Jake Spiddy said the girl was locked up whenever the trader went ashore. Sure enough, the next moment the face of the girl appeared framed in the ten-inch porthole and the Sea Fox found himself looking into a pair of large lustrous brown eyes which were shaded by a heavy wave of auburn hair hanging low down on her forehead. She looked at him for a long moment; then the nostrils of her straight, finely chiseled nose widened in a pant of gladness, and her red mouth smiled a welcome.

"Holy mack'rel!" the Sea Fox gasped under his breath. "If that

ain't a leetle o' the pootiest gal I ever see in all my born days."
Aloud he blurted, "Good afternoon, miss. I rather guess you're
the Ruth Delway Cap'n Skiddy was a-tellin' me about."

"Yes, and I just know you're Captain Pepper!" she flashed
back, her smile breaking into a little laugh of delight.

She attempted to get her head farther out of the porthole and
in so doing exposed to view a chin which for depth and breadth
would have done credit to an Amazon queen.

"By gum! I don't believe no female with a chin like that ever
lost her mind for a single minnit," he decided, mentally surveying this mark of an indomitable will with some slight misgivings.

But he could detect no flaw in the story she told him—essen-
tially the same as already related by Jake Spiddy—of how she
came aboard the hulk under the care of old man Graggs. And
through all her talk there breathed a fervent desire to go home
to her people. Yet somehow, despite her apparent sincerity, the
Sea Fox could not crush out the feeling that there was something
spurious about this lovely young woman.

"Very well, Miss Delway," he said at length. "I'll see that ye get
home. Now I'll jes' slip over to the ship for a few things I'll need
to get ye outa that wagon an' I'll be back soon's I can."

"You won't fail me, Captain Pepper?" Ruth entreated, her
great eyes so melting in their appeal that for a moment or two
the Sea Fox felt a little ashamed of the plans quickening in his
brain.

"No fear," he assured her. "I'll look arter ye to the queen's taste.
Don't worry no more."

He cast off the painter and rowed back to his ship so wrapped
in a sudden intensity of reflection that he seemed unaffected by
the scorching African heat which had driven nearly every living
thing to the shade.

As the Sea Fox came over the rail Tom Dollar sauntered up,
mopping his lean countenance with a frayed bandanna handkerchief the size of a small tablecloth. He fixed his keen, smoky-
gray eyes on the skipper.

"What's in the wind, Cappen; might I ask?" he inquired.

The Sea Fox's black eye flared with amusement.

"A hull bar'l o' the devil's shakin's, I've a notion, Tom Dollar," and forthwith he told his trusted officer all about his transactions with Jake Spiddy and the girl. "Thar's an underhanded scheme on, Tom Dollar, I can feel it in my bones!" concluded the Sea Fox. "A nigger in the woodpile. Four hundered an' seven o' 'em, I shouldn't wonder."

While Tom Dollar chewed assiduously on his quid and turned the captain's statement over in his mind.

"If I ain't back here before dark with the gal you'll know that I'm bein' held aboard the hulk," the Sea Fox added. "But don't let that bother ye. You'll know then that he has double-crossed me an' is takin' my slaves an' also the five thousand dollars reward money for the gal."

"Hell's lifts!" protested Tom Dollar. "I wouldn't pay that sculpin a cussed red cent till I had all the slaves he promised ye aboard here an' the gal with 'em! He can't double-cross ye then."

" 'Tain't customary, Tom Dollar. Niggers has to be paid for on the nail. Many a skipper in days past has sailed away with a cargo o' slaves an' paid with the fore-tops'l. I'll have to pay Spiddy. An' so's he won't suspicion that I'm onto his tricks I'll give him the reward money, too. I'll get everythin' back again shortly, an' ye know, Tom Dollar, thar' ain't nothin' I enj'y more than pretendin' to fall inter the trap some enterprisin' cuss has laid for me. Now all ye have to do is to keep yer eyes continually on the *Horatio*. The minnit he starts takin' slaves aboard ye get our hundered slaves onto the *Wild Pigeon* quick's ye can and get ready for sea so's ye can foller the *Horatio* out. Never mind about me. I'll be on the job somewhere. Above all, don't forget to keep yer eyes on that hooker."

Going down into his cabin, the Sea Fox put a flat leather case into his pocket together with a derringer. Picking up a carpetbag he crammed $15,175 into it from the safe, working so expeditiously that inside of fifteen minutes he was going over the rail of the *Horatio* with the carpetbag. And in five minutes more he had paid Jake Spiddy the money for the slaves and advanced the reward for the girl.

Jake Spiddy gave the Sea Fox a receipt and an order on Mafuca Sanchez for the four hundred and seven slaves, stipulating however that the order should not be presented until Miss Delway was safely aboard the *Wild Pigeon,* for if by any chance the project miscarried he, Jake Spiddy, would return the money and keep the slaves.

"Waal, that's all fair 'nough, Cap'n Spiddy," agreed the Sea Fox. "I'm a-goin' arter the gal right now," and forthwith he got into his dinghy.

Jake Spiddy grinned and with a peculiar glitter in his eyes watched the little slaver shove off.

A WHITE rounded arm waved a greeting from the port-hole as the Sea Fox drew up to the mizzen chains, and with a word of encouragement to Ruth he climbed aboard the hulk. He observed that the *Break of Dawn* had a flush deck which was littered amidships with hen-coops and broken cases.

Hearing snores issuing from the trade-room abaft of the main-mast, the Sea Fox glided softly to the open door and, peeking in, saw the fat Mpongwe clerk stretched out full length on the trade table, his head pillowed on a roll of calico and sound asleep. There was nothing to fear from him and so, losing no time, the Sea Fox descended the companion-ladder and went into the main cabin. It was nearly as hot as a bake-oven in the box-shaped apartment, although the skylight was wide open and there was an awning over the quarter. But the Sea Fox, eager to play his part, hardly noticed it.

Whipping a bunch of keys from his pocket and selecting a pass-key, he strode to the door of the room in which Ruth was confined and in another moment had unlocked it. The girl came out, a smiling pattern of wholesome womanhood that actually seemed to light up the dingy old cabin. She thanked him effusively for returning so quickly, although the Sea Fox fancied that he could detect a touch of half-frightened exultation in her tone.

"I'll just step into my room and get a few things I need," she told him, "and then we'll leave this horrid old wreck."

Ruth went into a room on the port side and he could hear her moving about in there when suddenly there came the jar of a boat striking the gangway-ladder and presently the sound of a harsh, cracked voice at the door of the trade-room waking the clerk.

"Jes' what I cal'lated on!" muttered the Sea Fox, smiling grimly. "Ole Graggs musta been hidin' in the mangroves back o' the ship waitin' for me."

The girl of course had also heard the new arrival and she came scuttling from her room, her comely features expressing a lively dismay.

"Oh, goodness gracious!" she panted excitedly. "Mr. Graggs has come back for something or other. He's sure to come down here. Please go into that spare stateroom." She indicated a door near the entrance to the companionway. "He never goes in there. And I'll go back to my prison-room."

"What's the matter with me heavin' the ole goat in there an' lockin' him up? Then thar' won't be no delay," suggested the Sea Fox.

Ruth looked at him imploringly.

"No, no! Please don't mistreat Mr. Graggs," she pleaded. "You don't know how good he's been to me. He'll go ashore again in a few minutes, and then I'll let you out."

"But, Jumpin' Judith," he argued, "won't Graggs see my boat alongside an' suspect sunthin?" He was quite delighted at what he considered her fine acting.

"No," she assured him. "It's on the opposite side from the gangway, and he won't look round in all this heat. Please, please. Captain Pepper," she urged, as steps could be heard coming along the deck. "Mr. Graggs will be down here in a minnit. Go in that room, do!"

She almost shoved him through the door and, hastily closing it, turned the key in the lock in such a way, the Sea Fox noticed, that a key could not be inserted from the inside.

"That gal is as smart as she's pretty," he thought. "Shouldn't wonder if she was the brains o' the combination. Spiddy don't look like he had more'n a spoonful." The Sea Fox, with his ear pressed against the thick door, could hear nothing save the faint sound of guarded voices somewhere in the cabin. He left the door and looked at his watch. It was five minutes past three. By the time Jake Spiddy got the slaves aboard and the wind and tide served it would be nearly two o'clock the next morning before the *Horatio* sailed.

"They aim to keep me here until the vessel is clear o' the coast, an' then I s'pose old Graggs'll show up with some cut an' dried yarn or other an' let me out." He looked at the massive teak door. "Solid's a rock," he muttered. "It'ud take a man ten years to cut aroun' that lock. Good thing I allus go equipped for jes' sech emergencies as this here."

He drew the flat leather case from a pocket and, opening it, exposed part of a burglar's kit—a pair of keyhole pincers, two little saw-blades, files, and a bit of wire. Trying the pincers and finding that they fitted round the end of the key in the lock, the Sea Fox gave a satisfied grunt and restored the leather case to his pocket. He then crawled into the bunk and, stretching out on the bare mattress, whiled away the time with one of the intricate wire puzzles with which he was always provided against a spare moment. When it got too dark for this, he still lay in the bunk meditating over this fascinating situation.

Presently ascertaining that it was eight o'clock by feeling the hands of his watch, he slid from the bunk and put his eye to the keyhole but could make out nothing but a blur. Then, inserting the pincers, he gripped the key and easily unlocked the door. Turning the knob noiselessly, he slowly opened the door and, stepping out cautiously, heard a subdued exclamation of surprise at his side. Whirling on his heel, he looked into the wide, startled eyes of the girl.

A rocking-chair, still vibrating in the dim light of the turned down lamp, showed how hastily she had sprung to meet him.

"You—you mustn't come out yet, Captain Pepper," she whispered, her mouth close to his ear. "Mr. Graggs didn't go ashore again and so I've had no chance to let you out." She pointed across the cabin to a perpendicular streak of light visible through a partly opened door. "He's in there now!" she warned.

"Sorry, my dear gal, but I can't wait no longer on this here job," the Sea Fox answered. "I gotta get into gear right now!"

He leaped to Graggs' room and, slamming the door shut, swiftly turned the key in the lock. Followed a flood of invectives like the cackling of an old hen from the inside of the room which brought a pleased smile to the face of the Sea Fox.

"Thar," he remarked. "Graggs is accounted for. He ain't hurt, an' he don't know who done it nuther. Jes' like ye wanted it, ain't it, miss? Now we'll get under weigh outa this. Get yer hat an' let's go!"

"But—but," she stammered, drawing back. "I really don't know what to do. I—"

"No, this is somethin' ye never figgered on, my gal!" he told himself. "We ain't got no time to palaver," he interrupted. "The fust thing we know that bag o' bones in thar 'ul stick his head through the port and wake all creation with his troubles. Come now. We gotta go alongside the *Horatio* fust so's I can show Cap'n Spiddy I've reskied ye. That was part o' our bargain."

Upon mentioning the *Horatio* and Cap'n Spiddy, Ruth flashed a singular look at the Sea Fox and without further demur got her hat and went on the quarter with him.

The great African moon shouldered up behind Rombi Peak, making things almost as plain as day. The deck was deserted and, going to the rail, the Sea Fox was delighted to find his dinghy still fast to the mizzen-chains. Losing no time, he helped his fair companion into the boat and shoved off. Before he was half-way to the *Horatio* he could see that Jake Spiddy was already taking the slaves aboard; an empty slave-canoe was backing away from the gangway.

The Sea Fox smiled grimly. The slaves would be his eventually, and in the meantime Jake Spiddy was saving him canoe hire for them. Cap'n Pepper had laid his plans to a hair and felt that he was prepared for anything.

As he pulled alongside of the gangway and stood up to catch the ladder, the Sea Fox heard a roar of laughter from the sailors aboard, followed by the mate's declaration that he was the best man on the seven seas and could whip his weight in wildcats. The next moment the horribly writhing features of the drunk-mad Twigg appeared over the rail and, blindly thrusting a pistol straight out before him, he fired pointblank at the Sea Fox. The whip-like report was still echoing along the banks when, without so much as a groan, the noted slaver clasped a hand to his breast, flung the other high in the air and toppled over backward into the black, sullen river.

HORRORSTRUCK, THE girl stared down dumbly at the bubbles rising where the Sea Fox had sunk. The boat, left to itself, would have drifted away had not one of the crew thrown a boathook over the gunwale and pulled it up to the gangway.

Jake Spiddy, standing on the poop, had witnessed the tragedy. With a roar of mingled rage and dismay he bounded along the deck to where Twigg was glaring dazedly at the smoking pistol in his hand. Jake Spiddy knocked the weapon from his grasp and, catching him by the dungaree jumper, shook him like a terrier does a rat.

"Sweet Jeeroos-a-lam! You've made a hellova mess of things now," bellowed the skipper, "killin' the Sea Fox. If them New Yorkers on the *Wild Pigeon* ever larn about it they'll blow us outa water with that big battery of theirs. Damn ye, anyhow, for a crazy, meddlin', fool!"

"Some—somebody musta put a ball on top the powder!" whimpered the white-lipped Twigg, stunned into soberness. "I swar' I didn't, Jake. Hope t' die if I did!"

"How the hell d'ye know what ye done, full of that 'nigger sleep' mixture!" growled his brother, letting him go. "Now get them tops'ls loosed an' then heave short. We must get to sea the minnit the last slave is aboard. That bucko mate on the *Wild Pigeon* will be tearin' up all hell in the mornin' searchin' for his skipper."

Facing aft, Jake Spiddy saw the girl running up and down in the waist moaning and wringing her hands.

"Oh, but the Sea Fox was a man!" she burst out. "Nothing could stop him from getting me out of the fix he thought I was in. And he died trying to keep faith with me. Oh, oh, we wanted to match wits with him and we led him to his death."

"There, there, Beth," soothed Jake Spiddy, putting an arm about her shoulders, "don't take it so hard. Nobody knowed that Twigg had it in him to go roarin' mad."

The girl seemed not to hear him but jerked away and, bursting into tears, buried her face in her hands and hurried below to the cabin.

Naturally while this was going on all hands had been gathered round the scene of the tragedy. However, Tom Dollar, who had been watching the *Horatio* through a powerful glass, in accordance with the Sea Fox's orders, had seen all that occurred and had also observed something which those on the *Horatio*, being so preoccupied in the waist, did not see.

Tom Dollar shut the telescope with a bang and slammed Robin Hood, the bosun, on his huge shoulder.

"Hell's lifts!" he ejaculated. "I allus said the Sea Fox could act the quickest o' any man in a 'mergency, an' damn if this don't prove it. Heave short on yer chain, Robin Hood. We'll foller that there Jake Spiddy to sea, an' then if he don't get the surprise o' his life I'll kiss the fust clam I see."

THE NEXT morning, just as the African sun had unveiled its terrible splendor and set the blue sea quivering with its beams, the two slave vessels crossed the Calabar bar and the *Horatio* headed away to the southward, her skipper becoming decidedly uneasy when he saw the *Wild Pigeon* swing in behind him on the same course. In an attempt to get away from this persistent and dangerous neighbor, Jake Spiddy kept off dead before the wind and crowded on every stitch of canvas his old brig could carry. But the *Wild Pigeon* also altered her course and, setting t'gallant and topmast stuns'ls, came up hand over hand on the *Horatio's* quarter.

Tom Dollar then reduced sail so as to regulate his speed with the other vessel's. As the *Wild Pigeon* forged up to within easy speaking distance, Jake Spiddy noticed, with no little apprehension, that her long thirty-two pounder swivel-gun amidships was trained on the *Horatio* and the gun-crew standing by it.

"Ahoy, the brig!" shouted Tom Dollar, taking off his hat politely to the girl, who stood near Jake Spiddy.

"What d'ye want?" barked the skipper.

"Jes' wanta ask a question or two," rejoined Tom Dollar, replacing his hat airily. "Didn't my skipper buy them slaves ye got aboard there?"

"Sweet Jeeroos-a-lam!" Jake Spiddy gave a scornful snort. "But that's a hell-ova thing to ask. In course he didn't!"

"Ye're a goldinged liar, Jake Spiddy, an' ye know it!" roared the Sea Fox, rolling out from under the spare boat on top of the after house, where he had lain concealed all the while.

Instantly his eye fell on the girl, standing close to the rail.

"Lower away yer yawl, Tom Dollar!" he shouted. "An' stan' by to pick up me an' a lady passenger!"

Like a hawk swooping, he seized the startled girl by her slim waist, and, before Jake Spiddy or any of his crew had recovered from their paroxysm of surprise at seeing this man like one risen from the dead, the Sea Fox had gathered her in his arms and leaped into the sea.

Masterly handled by Tom Dollar, the light sails seemed actually to melt from the yards of the *Wild Pigeon* so rapidly were they taken in. Her great fore tops'l was backed, checking her headway, while at the same time she dropped a boat in the water.

Five minutes later the dripping girl, laughing half-hysterically, was being helped by the Sea Fox up the side-ladder onto the deck of his ship.

Jake Spiddy, recovering from his amazement, ripped out an oath, slammed his hat onto the deck, jumped on it flat-footed, and strode foaming to the rail.

"Hey, ye damn idjuts!" he shouted at the top of his voice: "Bring that woman back here. That's my wife, blast ye!" He waved his long arms frantically.

"I knowed all along the gal was sunthin' to ye," responded the Sea Fox blandly. "I jes' brought her aboard here to keep her outa harm's way, Cap'n Spiddy, for I'm a-goin' to begin tossin' iron from my guns inter ye if ye don't start movin' them slaves aboard here, an' that five thousand dollars reward money too!"

As Jake Spiddy threw a murderous look at the *Wild Pigeon's* heavy guns and the determined looking slavers standing by them, little Twigg errupted from the companionway, the bottle of "nigger-sleep" in one hand and the pistol in the other. Rushing to the rail, he threw them overboard. Then he doffed his cap in a wide arc to the Sea Fox.

"That's the stuff that made me sky-blue-pink," he piped out. "I never saw ye when I fired that time, Cap'n Pepper. Hope t'die if I did. I knowed I never loaded the pistol with ball, but I might sometime if I kept on drinkin' that stuff. No more for me."

"Amen!" murmured Mrs. Spiddy fervently, a thankful look leaping into her eyes, which the Sea Fox immediately noted.

"I b'lieve ye, mister," rejoined the latter. "But, as 'twas, ye worked right inter my hand by firin' at me. My intentions was to pretend to fall outa the boat, when I came alongside with Mrs. Spiddy, an' let ye think I was drownded while in the confusion that 'ud nat'rally follow I'd swim under water to yer starn, climb aboard an' stow away. Which I did, but shootin' at me made my dis'pearance more nat'ral like, d'ye see."

"But, Captain Pepper, how did you know that I wasn't Ruth Delway?" flashed Mrs. Spiddy. "You told me from the very first that you had never seen her."

"How'd ye hear 'bout Ruth Delway?" countered the Sea Fox.

"Through Mr. Graggs. He's a distant relative of my husband's, and we were so frightfully short of provisions aboard the *Horatio* that I was staying aboard the hulk while we lay in Calabar. It was the trader who hatched the scheme to make you think I was the lost girl and the rest of it."

"H-mm! I knowed you was new to this part o' the coast by yer actions," mused the Sea Fox. "Whar' ye fell down was in placin' too much dependence on the gossip o' an ole dotard like Graggs. He never saw Cap'n Delway or his wife, or he'd a-knowed, same's I did, that the darter he lost couldn't be a scrumptious gal like ye be, for"—his massive features broadened into a smile—"the Delways was Haitians an' black's the inside o' the cook's funnel."

"Oh!" gasped Mrs. Spiddy faintly, her firmly moulded chin sagging.

"Sweet Jeeroos-a-lam!" roared Jake Spiddy from his poop, uneasy over a conversation he could not hear. "Don't stan' there palaverin' with my wife. I'm the one to blame for this shindig. Take yer slaves an' gold, Cap'n Pepper, an' be damned to you!"

"I'll do that in a jiffy, Cap'n Spiddy," responded the Sea Fox blandly. "An' thank ye kindly for fixin' it so that I've saved a month's time." He turned to his lovely guest. "Meantime, Mrs. Spiddy, please to set in that chair by the scuttlebutt an' I'll have the steward bring ye some refreshments like."

The vessels were then arranged so that the slaves could step from one to the other.

INSIDE OF two hours the last slave was under the *Wild Pigeon's* hatches, and the canvas bag containing the five thousand dollars had been dropped hastily into the hands of the Sea Fox by the awed Twigg, who immediately scampered back aboard his ship again.

As the Sea Fox escorted Mrs. Spiddy to the rail, she paused and held out her hand with a wan smile.

"I'm sorry, awfully sorry, Captain Pepper, I've made you all this trouble. Really I am!"

"Sho! No trouble 'tall, Mrs. Spiddy," he assured her, squeezing her plump hand. "I've enj'yed this leetle claw to wind'ard immensely. Besides y'know ye helped me to get away from the coast a month quick'n I could otherwise, d'ye see. An'," he added earnestly, "you've helped me more'n ye'll ever know. I heerd what ye said when ye thought I was killed. Yer heart's in the right place yet, Mrs. Spiddy. 'Twas poverty made ye desprate, I know. Consekently 'tain't right to let a smart, eddicated gal like ye go back to the coast broke. This here 'ull start ye goin' again." He shoved the bag of gold hurriedly into her hands. "Now go aboard yer ship an' show that husband o' yourn the error o' his ways. Good-by an' the hull ocean o' luck to ye!"

The girl looked down at the fortune in her hands and then, her brown eyes wet with tears, she threw her arms, bag and all, about the bull-neck of the grizzled Sea Fox and kissed him squarely on the mouth. The next moment she was running along the *Horatio's* deck to the poop.

Like one in an ecstatic dream the Sea Fox saw her waving a farewell hand as the vessels parted and filled away. Then, hearing a sudden, neighing snort right at his elbow, he turned and beheld Tom Dollar, whose lean features were screwed up into a multitude, of mirthful wrinkles.

"What ye standin' thar for, Tom Dollar, a-grinnin' like the ship's cat eatin' cheese out a can?" bristled the Sea Fox, shaking himself. "Show a leg an' set stuns'ls alow an' aloft. You'd never have a pooty gal smack ye one like that in a million years, Tom Dollar!"

The mate shook his long head.

"No wimmin' fur me, Cappen. Looks like I'm headin' fur the port of soot, sorrer, an' smoke fast 'nough as 'tis. Besides," he added, turning away to execute the order, "ye hain't got nothin' to brag 'bout, Cappen, as I can see. I could get the Queen o' Sheby to hug me nigh to death fur five thousand dollars."

SNARING THE SEA FOX

*The French thought they had him—this Sea Fox—
this little Yankee adventurer. And indeed it looked
as though he had at last been run to earth. For not
a gunshot off his* **Wild Pigeon's** *quarter the French
frigate* **Araignee** *thundered down the wind—and
ahead lay the dread reef called "Dutchman's Grave"!*

T HAT THICK, clammy mist peculiar to the Gulf of Guinea, which had enshrouded the French frigate *Araignee* during the night suddenly lifted about eight in the morning, disclosing on her starboard bow a large brigantine, well within gunshot, and heading into the coast under an immense press of canvas.

"A slaver bound into Old Calabar!" exclaimed Commodore Murat, a tall, stiff man with bushy black side-whiskers and eyes cold and gray as polished stone.

Focusing his glasses on the strange vessel he took a long look, swore softly beneath his breath, and turned again to his first lieutenant, who was new to the West African Coast.

"Mon Dieu! Mr. Lassan, that is the Yankee contraband-runner and slaver, the *Wild Pigeon,* the fastest keel on this coast— commanded by Captain Pepper—the Sea Fox, y' know—the most notorious smuggler in the trade and a man who is acknowledged to have no rival in the way of daring and success."

The commodore's agitation increased with his speech and he almost shouted, "Beat to quarters, Mr. Lassan, and give her a shot as soon as you can. The Sea Fox will doubtless engage us, for there is no surrender about him. He'll show fight, I'm sure!"

A hum of excitement ran through the thirty-two gun frigate as the men ran to quarters, for here was indeed a quarry worthy of any ship's metal. In another half-minute the frigate yawned slightly, a sheet of red flame issued from her starboard bowchaser followed by the sullen boom of a twenty-four pounder and a shot kicked up the spray close alongside of the *Wild Pigeon's* port quarter.

But contrary to the commodore's expectations, the Sea Fox made no hostile movement; holding his ship steadily on her course, her long, black, exquisitely proportioned hull cleaving the blue sea with all the grace and speed of a dolphin.

"Mon Dieu! He thinks he can escape from under my guns!" muttered the commodore, striding excitedly up and down the quarterdeck. "And he will, too," he added to himself, "if I keep off to bring my broadside to bear. I'll have to depend on my bow-chasers to wing him."

For a few minutes the black brigantine gradually increased her lead over the frigate, and the foaming bar of the Calabar River could be seen plainly about two miles ahead, when, of a sudden, the wind dropped to a faint zephyr. The slaver had run into a nearly calm streak. And while they were fanning across this the *Araignee,* which still held the wind, was overhauling them hand over hand and already her shots were spraying the water all about the contraband-vessel. But as yet no shot had struck her and this fact awakened a suspicion in the mind of the commodore. It suddenly dawned upon him that possibly the Sea Fox had sympathizers aboard the frigate. Then he remembered that among his crew were some men of the wrecked French brig *L'Aigle* whom the Sea Fox, at imminent risk of being captured meanwhile, had rescued and taken into Ayudah, nine months ago.

"Mr. Lassan," ordered the commodore dryly, "have the men serving the guns relieved and see if the firing is not more accurate!"

It seemed to be, but just as a shot tore through the second reef-band of the smuggler's mains'l she got the wind again, a sweet, strong breeze from the eastward. But it came too late. The frigate was now too close for the Sea Fox to hope to escape by depending on the speed of his craft alone. Realizing this, the *Wild Pigeon's* foremost hands—thirty seasoned ocean-scamps—looked inquiringly aft at their famous leader.

The Sea Fox regarded them with his curiously unflinching black eye—he had but one—and waved his hand in a reassuring gesture, his rugged, powerful features lighted by a smile. In the midst of this danger, imminent and threatening, which would have broken the spirit of a less resolute man he seemed actually happy.

Turning his short, thickset figure to windward the Sea Fox took a squint at the *Araignee* soaring down, her grinning guns run out, and gave a rapid order to Tom Dollar, the long, lanky mate, who immediately left the poop, a wide grin on his leathern countenance.

PULSES LEAPING with the fever of the chase so that he could hardly hold the glasses to his eyes, Commodore Murat saw the *Wild Pigeon*, of a sudden, yaw wildly and then come staggering up into the wind, while her sheets and braces were let fly. The next instant her crew began running along the decks, dragging long poles which they flung over the side and began pushing on frantically.

"Hurrah, hurrah, Mr. Lassan!" exploded the commodore in a very frenzy of delight. "The clever Sea Fox is caught at last! He's gone aground on 'The Dutchman's Grave,' part of the Bakasi Banks. I didn't think it ran out quite this far, though. See they are trying to shove the vessel off. Ha-ha, much good it will do them.

We—" He broke off suddenly, his face blanching as he gave an apprehensive glance at his three soaring steeples of canvas and then across the long green swells to where the breakers were blossoming white as they boomed on the yellow African sands.

"Mon Dieu! We're not sure of the water under us either, Mr. Lassan!" he interjected hurriedly. "We might go aground, too. Hard down your wheel and let her come to the wind. Back your main-yard!"

These orders were executed in a twinkling and the first lieutenant sought the commodore for further instructions.

"Man first, second, and third cutters, Mr. Lassan!" he directed, "and pull over to the slaver and take her by boarding. If the Sea Fox attempts to repel you, tell him unless he desists you will draw your boats out of the line of fire and signal the frigate to give him a broadside. But in any case he can't escape. See how vainly his crew are trying to shove her off with the poles!"

Mr. Lassan smiled at his volatile commander, who was so delighted at cornering the great Sea Fox that he was now actually doing a little dance-step.

In three minutes the same number of boats were dropped into the water, each one full of bluejackets armed with pistol and cutlass. They had hardly gotten a cable's length away from the frigate, however, when the commodore's face underwent a frightful contortion as he saw the slavers suddenly drop their poles overboard and make a dash for the running-gear. In another minute the beautiful brigantine with every stitch of canvas set was flying like a monstrous albatross over the rippling sea for the bar, now about a mile and a half distant.

"Tricked, by God, tricked!" bellowed the commodore like a bull in pain and slammed his glasses to the deck with such violence that the lenses flew about the deck. "That damned Sea Fox wasn't aground at all—he just pretended to be so as to render us temporarily helpless!"

Commodore Murat's lips trembled so with impotent rage that it was all he could do to stutter the order to recall the boats and then fill the yards. But all this took precious time, as the Sea Fox had very nicely calculated, and before the frigate was again in pursuit the black brigantine was safely out of gunshot.

"The game is not played out yet, sir," ventured the first lieutenant. "Look at the bar! It would be next to madness for the Sea Fox to attempt it, sir!"

HOPE INDEED revived in the breast of the fuming, commodore as he scanned the bar. It was one boiling mass of surf; great green billows rolling in and breaking on it and filling the air with spume. Would the Sea Fox dare to take his vessel through that maelstrom or wait until slack water when the bar could be navigated in comparative safety? If the Sea Fox decided to wait, as it appeared he must, there was a chance for the frigate to work inshore and take the brigantine by boarding.

But in another minute the commodore got an inkling of the desperate nature of the man he was endeavoring to capture. Through another pair of glasses he saw the Sea Fox being lashed to the wheel. Her crew then sprang upon the sheerpoles and clustered in the lower rigging. Not a halliard or sheet was started.

Breathlessly the men on the *Araignee* watched as the *Wild Pigeon,* her broad canvas wings stretching far out over the boiling water and towering in graceful symmetry to the blue African sky, hurled herself into the flying spume.

The Sea Fox was steering her like a thread through a needle and both skipper and ship were getting the bath of their lives. For part of the time the green, white-maned sea-horses were racing over her decks almost to the top of her bulwarks. Then the noble craft would shake herself, rise on a monstrous billow, her long polished hull shooting out of water until nearly half her keel, with the bright copper sheathing flashing in the sun, was visible. Then she would be buried again leaving nothing to be discerned but two snowy canvas spires rushing through acres of foam and the man-of-war hawks circling and dodging those sky-scraping trucks and screaming their exultation. One minute more and the *Wild Pigeon* had crossed the bar without parting so much as a ropeyarn.

An involuntary murmur of admiration came from nearly three hundred throats aboard the frigate as the *Wild Pigeon* shot into smooth water and trimmed her yards for the run up the river to Old Calabar (Duketown). She was safe now in the territory of Duke Ephraim, king of Calabar. Two hours later the *Wild Pigeon* was snugly moored in the midst of thick mangroves, close to the slave-*barracoons,* and about a quarter-mile above Duketown.

I N A black and brooding silence Commodore Murat watched the Yankee brigantine until she melted into the shadows of the high wooded banks. Then he gave orders for the frigate to haul her wind and lay off and on until the turn of the tide. After which he strode into his cabin his eyes glaring from under the frowning brows like those of a madman's.

"I'll be ruined—ruined!" he grated, slamming his gold-banded cap onto the table. "Yes, I'm done for if the Governor of San Luiz ever learns of the manner in which I've been outmaneuvered by that devilish Yankee." In a sudden fury he dashed his fist onto the polished mahogany: *"Mon Dieu!* I will become the laughingstock of the squadron. I might possibly be court-martialed! The one thing that will save me now is to capture the Sea Fox. He must leave this river in irons, my prisoner!"

Late in the afternoon the *Araignee* sailed up the river, and rounding-to in a direct line with the King of Calabar's English house, let go her anchor.

"I shall have to set a snare for that Sea Fox," the commodore confided to his first lieutenant. "Match cunning with cunning so to speak." He let his eyes rove over the town of palm-thatched huts, shaded by great tamarinds and coco-palms, until they rested on a thatched-over hulk moored to a bamboo-landing, and flying the French flag from her stub of a mizzen-mast.

"There is Trader Target's hulk over yonder," he mused. "He is a Frenchman transacting business under our flag. If the Sea Fox should set foot aboard there he would be in French territory in a manner of speaking. Hm, we shall see!"

"You mean, sir," asked the first officer, looking puzzled, "that you can't arrest the Sea Fox anywhere else but on the hulk?"

"Exactly. You see that while we are negotiating with Duke Ephraim for those Ibinku concessions, we naval commanders have orders not to molest any vessels trading in his territory unless they are known beyond doubt, to have slaves actually aboard. And I wouldn't care to take the responsibility of arresting the Sea Fox even on the hulk but for the fact that he is an escaped convict."

"An escaped convict!" echoed Mr. Lassan. "Why how could that be, sir."

"Oh, you haven't heard. Well a little over two years ago one of the squadron found him aboard of a French slaving schooner coming down the coast and the judge at San Luiz sentenced him to ten years in the Brest prison. He served five months and then escaped in some mysterious fashion. There is still a reward of five thousand dollars for his capture!"

"That being the case," decided Mr. Lassan, "I doubt very much whether such a clever rogue will ever step foot on the hulk while we are here."

Commodore Murat shrugged his shoulders. "I doubt it myself. But I'll set my trap aboard of the hulk nevertheless. There is a bare chance the Sea Fox may step into it. He's reckless enough to do most anything." He paused and slammed his fist into the open palm of his left hand, "But I'll get him eventually. Listen, Mr. Lassan. Rear-Admiral Fusenot, the Governor of San Luiz y'know, is bound down the coast on a dispatch-boat on his way here. A Mpongwe runner reported him a little to the north of the Bonny River yesterday. That means he'll probably be here sometime on Sunday, the day after tomorrow. Well, as soon as he clinches this concession with Duke Ephraim I shall have a free hand and I'm then going to throw a boarding-party aboard the *Wild Pigeon* and take the Sea Fox prisoner at all hazards.

Remember he is an escaped convict and wanted by the French Government."

THAT NIGHT the Sea Fox had two visitors. The first to arrive was the Mpongwe named Krinji, the river pilot and chief of the Egbo spies for Duke Ephraim. Besides speaking all the native dialects, he understood English, French, and naturally Spanish, the language of the coast. That Krinji could speak French was an accomplishment the commodore little dreamed the pilot possessed and he had carried on the conversation with his first lieutenant, outlining his plans, unguardedly in the presence of the spy, who was standing at the time nearby, apparently unconcerned, gazing over the muddy river. Forthwith Krinji made the Sea Fox acquainted with the commodore's scheme and then departed hurriedly to amuse himself with the gathering in front of the evening bonfire in the square by the palaver house.

Twenty minutes later the next visitor boarded the *Wild Pigeon* and was warmly greeted by the Sea Fox and Tom Dollar. It was Trader Target from the hulk, a thin, tired-looking man with a kindly cast of countenance. He sank into a chair opposite the Sea Fox at the latter's invitation.

Clearing his throat the trader said finally, "I've come to tell you that Commodore Murat put five of his Senegalese, disguised as Kroomen, aboard my hulk not an hour ago. I suppose you know what he did that for, Captain Pepper?"

"To be sure I do," said the Sea Fox, twirling his inevitable quill toothpick. "He's setting a snare for me. Thank ye for coming over an' tellin' me."

"Why shouldn't I? I haven't forgotten the time three years ago when that fire burned me out how you lent me the money and goods to start and—"

"Oh, belay that, Target!" interjected the Sea Fox reddening. "We can live but once, d'ye see. Tell me about the commodore. Guess he's all het up over that leetle trick I showed him this mornin'." The Sea Fox chuckled reminiscently.

The trader leaned over in his chair and lowered his voice.

snap them on his wrists. The Sea Fox then unwound a piece of fishline from the top button of his waistband. In the end of the line was a running bowline which he slipped down over the spindle of the lock in one of the cuffs and pulling back on the line with his teeth he drew the bolt. The handcuff slackened on his wrist and he slipped his hand out and went to work on the remaining iron. In less than three minutes from the time the irons were put on him the Sea Fox was free.

"Hell's lifts!" exclaimed the admiring Tom Dollar. "Ye did that slick's a whistle, cap'n. But, say, s'pose they ain't got them kind o' irons on the frigate. 'Twould be hell to pay an' no pitch hot!"

"The *Araignee* uses the same kind," the skipper assured him. "Trader Target told me. But I'll take a bit of wire along in case. Now comes the principal part, Tom Dollar."

He stripped off his upper garments to the skin and then had the mate strap a short, double-barreled pistol underneath the upper part of his right arm close to the armpit in such a way that when the arm was extended, as it would be if the Sea Fox was searched for weapons, it was entirely free from contact with the body.

The Sea Fox put on his clothes and looked at his watch.

"Eight o'clock, Tom Dollar. Time I was goin'."

They went on deck and Robin Hood, the Negro bosun, brought the dinghy to the gangway.

"You know what to do, Tom Dollar," said the Sea Fox, "whether I weather this thing or not. An' if I don't come back at the time specified, jes' give my regards to the boys in the Astor House bar an' buy 'em a drink for me."

Drawing a deep breath he shook hands with Tom Dollar, gave a long look alow and aloft at his beloved vessel, climbed down into the dinghy, and was rowed over the river to the bamboo landing.

Sending Robin Hood back with the boat the Sea Fox walked rapidly up to the hulk. Coming to the gangladder, he mounted this jauntily and leaped over the rail. His feet had hardly touched the deck when nine men, among whom he recognized one with the epaulets of a lieutenant, rushed out of the shadowed bulwarks and surrounded him, their drawn cutlasses gleaming in the starlight.

"Jumpin' Judith, lufftenant!" laughed the Sea Fox. "This here is a reg'lar surprise, ain't it. An' cussed if ye ain't got a reg'lar boardin' party. I ain't that tough be I?"

"Glad to see you take it this way, Captain Pepper," rejoined Mr. Lassan, his fine features brightening. "Rather have taken you on the high seas, though. Now, sergeant," he motioned to the sergeant of marines, who advanced and snapped a pair of handcuffs on the Sea Fox's wrists. The latter noted with no little satisfaction that they were of the same pattern as the ones he had experimented with.

The Sea Fox was then put into the cutter lying on the outside of the hulk, and in another ten minutes he was set aboard the frigate and ushered into the presence of the commodore. Murat was striding up and down on the thick cabin-carpet, under the brilliant rays of a big chased silver hanging lamp, and there was a look more of relief than triumph in his eyes as they fell on the little prisoner.

"So, Captain Pepper," he began smilingly, "you've decided to pay me a visit at last. Delighted to entertain you, I'm sure." He turned to the lieutenant. "You have searched him, I presume."

"Yes sir," said Mr. Lassan, and laid on the table the derringer and pen-knife he had taken from the slaver's pockets.

"Sure that is all, Mr. Lassan? We can't be too careful, y'know."

He went up to the Sea Fox and deftly patted his clothing from head to foot, the slaver meanwhile smiling and extending his arms apparently to facilitate the search.

"Very good, Mr. Lassan, your work was thorough. You may leave the prisoner with me, I will assume personal charge of him."

THE OFFICER saluted and withdrew with his men. The commodore closed the door, and coming back, said, "*Mon Dieu,*

Captain Pepper! You have the reputation of being so clever. Is it possible you were not aware that Trader Target's hulk was French territory?"

Raising his manacled hands the Sea Fox fished a toothpick from the pocket of his pongee shirt, placed it in his mouth and smiled a little ruefully.

"To be sure I knowed it was, commodore, but Duke Ephraim give me to understand that ye wouldn't molest me while I was in the river unless, in course, I was takin' natives aboard."

"Nor would I had you been a mere slaver, Captain Pepper. Evidently you forgot that you are an escaped convict. No agreement we have with the king provides for the immunity of such as you."

"Guess ye win, all right," conceded the Sea Fox. "But thar's jes' one thing I'd like to know. Did Target take any part in settin' that snare for me?"

"No, no, how could you possibly think that?" said the commodore hurriedly. "I've had men aboard the hulk since the night of the day on which you arrived."

"Glad to hear that," said the Sea Fox. "I allus regarded Target as a friend, d'ye see. And," he added mentally, "Target will get his wine-shop in France." After a little pause he said, "If ye don't mind, commodore, I'd like to turn in somewhere. I've had ruther a busy day an' in course I never suspected this."

"Just a moment, captain, and I show you your room." The commodore went to a desk, pulled open a drawer, and took out a pair of shiny new handcuffs. To his dismay the Sea Fox saw that they were Poullet's patent. It would take him at least two hours to pick those locks with the wire he had concealed in his trousers waistband.

Commodore Murat snapped them on his wrists. "Double-irons for you, Captain Pepper. Your ability is too well known for you to be trusted with ordinary handcuffs. Now come with me."

He flung open the door of a stateroom and motioned the Sea

Fox to enter. The latter found himself in a splendidly furnished little cabin with a deep wide berth.

"Get all the rest you can, my dear captain," advised the commodore. "Rear-Admiral Fusenot, the Governor of San Luiz, will be aboard tomorrow, and I want you to look well when you meet him."

"Thanks," smiled the little smuggler. "I'll try an' give him a hearty greeting."

"That is the proper spirit, Captain Pepper," approved the commodore, and bidding his prisoner good-night, he locked the door carefully.

A LONG about sundown, the following afternoon, the Sea Fox pricked up his ears at the sound of an unusual briskness over his head on the deck.

"Jumpin' Judith!" he exclaimed, "Here comes the Gov'nor of San Luiz or I'm a Dutchman!"

BOOM! The frigate trembled to the recoil of a twenty-four-pounder. Ten more guns were fired one after another, the eleven-gun salute accorded a visiting rear-admiral, and the Sea Fox knew that his surmises were correct.

"Now let's see," mused the Sea Fox. "I know the habits o' these navy folks pretty well an' I figger that the Gov'nor will have dinner fust, and arter his bilges is comfortably awash with champagne, he'll want to have a look at yours truly. Waal, I'll be ready fur him."

Cap'n Pepper glanced down at the double-irons on his wrists and chuckled. At the three meals served to him that day in his room the commodore and master-at-arms had been present and the commodore himself had relocked the irons when the prisoner had finished eating. And even an expert could not have told, unless he had taken the locks of the Poullet cuffs apart, that they had been tampered with in such a way that it only required a jerking movement of the wrists to spring them.

As the Sea Fox had conjectured, when dinner was over and cigars lighted, the Governor proposed to the commodore that they have a look at the famous prisoner. It was then just eight-fifteen by the cabin clock and a minute later the Sea Fox was aroused by the turning of the key in the lock and as the door swung open wide he found himself confronted by the commodore and a short, thick-set man with a square, broad-boned face and restless gray eyes. This little man was all rigged out in the bullion epaulets and gold buttons of a rear-admiral and wore a glittering star on his left breast. Of course the Sea Fox needed no one to tell him that he was looking at the governor of San Luis.

Elevating his eye-glasses the governor surveyed the prisoner for a long moment in much the manner of one inspecting some strange wild animal at the zoo, and then observed, "So this is that clever American slaver is it; h—mm. Commodore Murat, permit me to congratulate you on this capture. You have performed a signal service and I shall emphasize that fact in my dispatches which I am forwarding soon to the Admiralty."

He had a high, squeaky voice which struck the Sea Fox as being strangely odd, issuing from that deep chest.

Turning from the beaming commodore, the governor addressed the prisoner, "You may come out into the cabin, my man. There are some questions I should like to ask you. You of course may answer at discretion."

The Sea Fox bowed and followed them into the luxurious apartment paneled in rosewood and mahogany and stood as far away from the direct rays of the great hanging lamp as he could.

The two officers seated themselves near the center-table and the Governor began, "If you should tell us how you managed to escape from the prison at Brest, Captain, doubtless you will be treated less rigorously when you are placed on trial."

The Sea Fox smiled and advanced two steps toward them.

"Ye wanta know, I take it, jes' what means I employed to break jail, Gov'nor?"

"Quite right, my man," said the governor graciously, scenting a confession.

"I escaped somethin' like this!" said the Sea Fox, his voice low and vibrant with lethal earnestness.

THE WORDS had hardly left his lips when to the officers' surprise and horror the shackles flew from his wrists and a double-barreled pistol leaped from some part of his clothing into his hand, the polished steel bores pointed directly at them.

"One yelp out o' ye for help an' ye are dead meat," he warned them. "Ye know me!"

Indeed they did know him. And they sat motionless, recalling vividly to mind the many instances of the terrific power which this little man by sheer force of character had exerted over his enemies.

"I see ye prefer to live," observed the Sea Fox smiling grimly. "Now, commodore, pick up them handcuffs an' iron yerself an' the gov'nor, cross-fashion. Ye know how it's done. Better be quick about it, too, afore I go sorta crazy an' start shootin' regardless."

"For God's sake, commodore!" muttered the governor, the color of ashes. "Do as he tells you. His eye is glaring like a maniac's already!"

Like one in a trance the commodore obeyed, and when the irons were on the Sea Fox stepped up and rapped the locks of the Poullet cuffs smartly with the butt of his pistol, thus resetting the springs with which he had tampered.

"Good enough!" approved the Sea Fox. "Now kindly march into that room I stayed in."

When they were in the room the Sea Fox said: "I don't wanta be too harsh with ye gentlemen. I s'pos I oughta gag ye but if ye'll give me yer word o' honor ye won't call for help inside o' a half-hour I won't humiliate ye that way."

"You have my word for it," promptly replied the Governor. "If I were gagged I'd be suffocated in no time. I can't breathe through my nose."

"How about ye, commodore? Gimme yer word?" asked the Sea Fox.

In a sullen tone the commodore agreed and the slaver locked them in the room. Then he crossed to the portieres at the back of the cabin and swept them back, disclosing a solid bulkhead.

"Here," the Sea Fox told himself, his heavy jaws clamping on his toothpick. "Here is where I've slipped. But I couldn't have foreseen this, nohow."

The bulkhead had been built in back of the gun-ports since Trader Target had visited the cabin and he had told the Sea Fox that he would have an unobstructed access to the ports. The slaver's original plan had been to overcome the commodore and then slip overboard out of one of the stern ports and swim to an old dismantled bark belonging to Duke Ephraim, anchored about a hundred yards down the river, where he would find a canoe waiting to convey him to the *Wild Pigeon*. Now the only way to get to the ports would be to leave the commodore's cabin, pass the sentry at the door, and also pass in plain sight of the officers in the ward-room before he reached the alley-way. Quite out of the question.

"Pepper," the Sea Fox told himself. "Ye are in a hell of a fix. Ye'll have to do some tall scratchin' to get outa this hole, an' that's a fact."

And then through an open door of a stateroom, the one allotted to the Governor, he caught sight of the rear-admiral's gold-laced chapeau and a cloak hanging against the bulkhead.

TEN MINUTES later the sentry before the door froze into attention and saluted as the governor passed him hurriedly and made for the gangway. The junior officer on watch espied the cocked hat and naval cloak by the light of the gangway-lantern and hurried up to him in some trepidation, for the little governor was known to be rather eccentric in his ways.

"Lieutenant," snapped the governor in his high squeaky voice, his face averted over the gangway. "Dispense with all ceremony and get a boat here for me as quickly as possible. It is imperative that I see the King of Calabar at once."

He spoke in Spanish but the officer attributed this to the fact that as there were men about he didn't wish them to know the business he was going on.

In a twinkling a boat was gotten ready and the governor in almost indecent haste for one of his standing hurried down the gangladder, got into the boat and gave the order to shove off. Eight minutes later the governor was stepping ashore on the landing and without so much as a word to the boat-crew he scampered away and vanished amidst a group of palms.

"Queer old coot, that governor," commented one of the sailors. "I've an idea he's about half-seas over. Did any of you notice he ain't got no coat on under that cloak. His hat was wrong side first and damned if he wasn't wearing his sword on the starboard side. Must be pretty drunk, eh, mates?"

Presently the eyes of the officer on watch on the *Araignee* nearly popped from his head as he saw the *Wild Pigeon,* her towering canvas like two peaks of snow in the moonlight, come flying down the river. The officer at once sounded the general alarm, but it being Sunday night, the weekday discipline had been relaxed and before the singing, wine-drinking crew could respond and go to their stations the brigantine was upon them.

The next instant an electric thrill went through the ship's complement as the sultry African river suddenly reverberated to the roar of an eighteen-pounder close aboard. The *Wild Pigeon* was merely giving a parting salute, however—a blank charge— and immediately swerved back on her course like a gull dipping its wing. And by the time the frigate's crew, working against wind and tide had hauled on the spring to their cable so as to get a broadside to bear the *Wild Pigeon,* going like a race-horse, had flashed out of sight behind the high bluffs of Dindo Point. She would, wind and weather permitting, never stop again this side of America.

While the first lieutenant was staring at the point where the slaver had vanished a quartermaster came up and reported that he had seen a little man wearing an admiral's cloak standing on the poop of the slaver and waving a gold-laced chapeau as she flew past.

Upon hearing this the first lieutenant was seized by a dread suspicion. Rushing down into the commodore's cabin and hearing some one kicking on the stateroom door his worst fears were realized as he unlocked it and beheld his two superiors shackled together—the governor minus his trousers.

On the table the Sea Fox had left a hasty scrawl addressed to Duke Ephraim and requesting him to reimburse the governor for the loss of his wearing apparel and the sword and to charge it to the Sea Fox's account.

The little governor read it and chuckled. Unlike the commodore, he was a good loser.

"Call him slaver, pirate, or what you will, commodore," he observed, "but I can't help feeling that there is something really great about a man who will take the chances he does. And another thing, commodore, there is no doubt but that he feels he is engaged in a worthy trade and that we have no right to interfere. But I think I shall take him up, after all, on his offer to buy me new trousers!"

ABOUT THE AUTHOR

COMRADES, HOWDY. I was born in Boston. At the age of eight began my first adventure by commandeering a lobster-man's dory one night and setting sail (in company with a lad a year younger) for what was then known as the Sandwich Islands. Half-way across Massachusetts Bay we ran out of provisions and my crew mutinied. At this critical juncture a lobster smack swooped down and towed us home.

I shall start on my last great adventure with a chuckle if I am able, for a moment, to picture the owner of the dory as I saw him on the afternoon of our return. He was dancing up and down the beach in a most unseemly manner for a man of sixty-three, one leg of his patched trousers outside his cowhide boot, beating the air with his fists and yelling like a maniac. Nothing saved my crew and me from being drawn and quartered on the spot but the opportune dropping of his upper set of false teeth, his long thin nose in imminent danger of being engulfed in the roaring cavern beneath. While he was fishing his teeth out of the sand we vanished homeward. Selah.

Eight years later shipped with J. William R. Wing of New Bedford for a whaling voyage in the Atlantic and Indian Oceans. Was thirty-nine months on that cruise. Then the merchant service. In the intervals beach-combing on the East coast of Africa; Chile; mate of a South Sea trader (the *Luka*); newspaper work in Cape Town and J'burg (too many rules); special service for U.S.; back to the merchant service and just at present I'm ashore in sight of San Francisco Bay for a while.

This is all about myself but I wish you would let me talk whale for a few minutes. A writer (I've forgotten his name and also the name of his book) has stated that the whale is the most harmless critter in the whole universe. Aforesaid whale being nothing more or less than an immense, sluggish mass of fat waiting out there in the ocean for some one to come up and stick him. Aha! Wait a minute, comrades, till I hone me iron; let him rant.

This wise knight of the keys further states that all these tales of hair-breadth escapes from infuriated whales are mere figments of some Ananias with designs on the shore-going public. Wise guy, that. All right, my iron's ready.

There is no question but that the baleen whale, such as the Greenland, the Right, the Blue, etc., are naturally timid and rarely put up a fight. But the giant sperm whale with his twenty-eight foot walking-beam of a lower jaw, armed with 43 sturdy ivory carrots nine inches long is, as many a vacant chair in the home of a whaling town can testify, the wickedest fighter in the world. The writer quoted made the mistake by saying *all* whales.

Out here in the West we have a black bear so mild and inoffensive that it is a common saying: "Ye kin walk up an' kick him in the stummick."

A certain tourist, hearing this, forthwith conceived a supreme contempt for *all* bears.

The neighbors shipped back to the tourist's widow all that they could find of his remains, bearing this tag:

"He kicked a grizzly in the guts."

—James K. Waterman